"Look at all these dresses," Samantha said, staring at the rows of wedding gowns that filled the Bridal Shoppe. "I never realized how many different kinds of wedding dresses there were to choose from." Rack after rack of gowns filled the store, in colors ranging from the purest white to the softest yellow. Toward the back of the store were rows of bridesmaid dresses in a rainbow of colors and dozens of styles.

Samantha pressed her hands to her head as she took in the huge display. "I couldn't pick one of these over another!" she exclaimed, fighting the urge to turn and flee the store. "Can't I just get married in jeans?"

"Absolutely not," Beth said firmly. "That's why I'm here. We're going to make sure you get the right dress."

"Good," Samantha said. "Because I don't have a clue as to what would be right for me."

THOROUGHBRED

BRIDAL DREAMS

CREATED BY

JOANNA CAMPBELL

WRITTEN BY

MARY NEWHALL

HarperEntertainment
An Imprint of HarperCollinsPublishers

HarperEntertainment
An Imprint of HarperCollins*Publishers*
10 East 53rd Street, New York, NY 10022-5299

Produced by 17th Street Productions,
an Alloy Online, Inc., company

HarperCollins books are available at special quantity discounts for bulk
purchases for sales promotions, premiums, or fund-raising.
For information please call or write:
Special Markets Department, HarperCollins Publishers Inc.,
10 East 53rd Street, New York, NY 10022-5299.
Telephone: (212) 207-7528. Fax: (212) 207-7222.

ISBN 0-06-059524-8

HarperCollins®, ®, and HarperEntertainment™
are trademarks of HarperCollins Publishers Inc.

Cover art © 2004 by 17th Street Productions,
an Alloy Online, Inc., company

First printing: June 2004

Printed in the United States of America

Visit HarperEntertainment on the World Wide Web at
www.harpercollins.com

❖ 10 9 8 7 6 5 4 3 2 1

For Joanna Campbell, who started it all.
Thanks, Joanna.

BRIDAL DREAMS

1

"WHAT A MESS," TOR NELSON SAID, HIS ARM AROUND HIS wife, Samantha. Tor and Samantha were standing in the doorway of the spare bedroom in their home at Whisperwood, the Kentucky eventing farm they owned. Late autumn sunlight shone through the window, and dust motes danced in the streaks of light, making the room look even dingier than it was.

"I don't know where to start." Samantha groaned, eyeing the piles of boxes that filled the room. "I didn't realize we'd accumulated so much stuff over the years."

Tor laughed, giving Samantha's long auburn curls a gentle tug. "That's because we spend all our time in the stables," he said. "We've been so busy running

1

Whisperwood that we haven't paid much attention to the house. When we don't know what to do with our junk, we throw it in here and shut the door, quick."

Samantha twisted her neck to eye her tall, blond husband. "At least you said *we* do that. I'd hate to think this clutter is all my doing." She looked back into the room and shook her head. "We're never going to get this room turned into a nursery in time."

Ever since last summer, when they had found out they were going to be parents, they had talked about turning the long-neglected storage room into a bedroom for the baby. But with all the things that needed to be done at the stable, the daunting project had been easy to postpone.

Tor gave Samantha's cheek a kiss, then reached in front of her to pat her round stomach. "I want you as content as an old broodmare," he said fondly. "I'll take responsibility for the whole room if it makes you happy." He leaned down and picked up a pair of discarded high-heeled shoes. "Yup," he said with a grin, dangling the dainty shoes by their heel straps, "I remember when I decided never to wear these again."

Samantha turned, snatched the shoes from his hand, and gave him a light smack on the shoulder.

"You are so silly," she said. "I threw these in here until I could find the time to put together the things that could go to the clothing bank. They're perfectly good shoes, but not for me. Give me a pair of paddock boots and some jeans and I'll be just fine." Then she looked around the room again and started to laugh. "In fact, I think half the things in here were supposed to be packed up for charity."

"And now it's going to happen," Tor replied. "Either that or we can turn one of the empty stalls into a nursery for little Horatio."

"Horatio?" Samantha rolled her eyes. "Yesterday it was Galileo, and the day before that you were calling the baby Ferdinand. Where do you come up with these goofy names?"

Tor shrugged. "I'm just working my way through the alphabet," he said. "My next name suggestion will have to start with an *I*."

"I think we'd better buy one of those name-the-baby books before you hit on some awful name that you actually like," Samantha said. "If you call our child Zelda, she just might want to live in the barn instead of in the house with us."

"Or we might end up with a son named Waldo," Tor said helpfully.

"Or a daughter named Mackerel? I don't think

so." Samantha turned back to the room and shuddered. "I guess we've put this off long enough," she said, taking a hesitant step into the crammed room. "Where did all this junk come from?"

"It's from six years of two hopeless pack rats sharing a house," Tor replied. "And from being busy making Whisperwood into the greatest sport horse farm on the East Coast."

Samantha looked over her shoulder to smile at Tor again. "We *have* done pretty well with training horses and teaching young riders how to compete in three-day eventing," she said with a smile.

"And don't forget using Finn to breed some excellent foals," Tor added. They had brought the big brown stallion from Ireland when they returned to the United States six years earlier. Finn McCoul's colts and fillies were doing well competing in dressage, arena jumping, and cross-country, helping to draw good publicity for the Nelsons' farm.

"Staring at this mess isn't getting anything done," Tor said, nudging Samantha further into the room. "We have only four months before little Igor is due. If we get started now, we might be able to empty the room out by then." He bowed low, sweeping his hand toward the floor. "Tell me where to begin, milady. I am at your service."

4

Before Samantha could reply, the doorbell rang. "Drat!" she exclaimed. "I was just getting up the nerve to open a box."

Tor took her by the shoulders and turned her toward the hallway that led to the living room and entryway of their one-story ranch-style house. "You go see who it is," he said. "I'll clear a trail in here so we can at least see a bit of the floor. That should give us some encouragement."

"Thanks, Tor," Samantha said gratefully, then hurried down the hall, relieved that she had been given a short reprieve.

When she swung the front door open, Ashleigh Griffin, her daughter, Christina Reese, and Samantha's younger sister, Cindy McLean, were standing on the porch. The three women, clad in jeans and old T-shirts, were all carrying large paper bags.

"We come bearing gifts," Ashleigh announced as Samantha stepped back to let them into the house.

"I know I should be appreciative," Samantha said hesitantly, looking at the bags, "but I'm trying to get stuff out of the house, not bring more in."

Cindy grinned. "We know," she said. "That's why we came." She nodded at the bag she was holding, her short blond hair bobbing in front of her face. "We're the three fairy godmothers. My gift is cleaning supplies. Things are quiet at Tall Oaks today, and I want to make sure my niece or nephew has the nicest possible room." Cindy, a retired jockey, was the head trainer and manager at Ben al-Rihani's stable, a well-known Thoroughbred breeding and training farm.

"Paint and wallpaper for the nursery," Christina informed Samantha, pointing at the bag she held. "We're ready to get to work. Just tell us where to start."

"Don't you have school today?" Samantha asked the younger woman.

"Just my morning class," Christina explained. At eighteen, Christina was an accomplished jockey, with wins in several prestigious races to her credit. Now she was attending the local community college, starting the classes she needed to earn a degree in veterinary medicine.

"And we brought food," Ashleigh, Samantha's close friend, said. "Deli sandwiches and everything from dill pickles to potato salad. We need to keep our strength up, you know."

Samantha smiled gratefully, touched by the thoughtfulness of her friends. "I do appreciate this," she said. "Tor's already starting on the room. Let's put the food in the kitchen, then we can go see what kind of progress he's made."

By the time Samantha led the way to the bedroom, Tor had moved several boxes against one wall, clearing the middle of the room.

"This is perfect," Ashleigh said. "We can go through the boxes and get things sorted out." She nodded confidently. "It won't take long with all of us working at it."

"Three categories," Cindy said with authority. "Keep, throw away, or give away." She looked at Samantha and narrowed her eyes. "And the keep pile can't be any bigger than the other two."

"Oh," Samantha said, twisting her mouth to one side. "You sound like you know what you're talking about."

Cindy nodded, bending down to open a box. "I do. Remember, I moved back here from New York less than a year ago. I spent eleven years in that apartment near Elmont, and it was crammed full. I got rid of a lot of stuff that I didn't have any use for. Now it's your turn."

Ashleigh sat on the floor and pulled the lid off another box. "Mike and I have been at Whitebrook for over twenty years," she said, referring to her husband, Mike Reese, and the nearby Thoroughbred breeding and training farm they owned. "I can't imagine the work it would take for us to move anything from there." She lifted a framed picture from the box and held it up. "This is a keeper," she announced.

"Sierra and Tor," Samantha said, taking the picture and admiring her handsome husband astride the big chestnut horse. "Look at how good you two looked going over that jump. Do you remember that steeplechase, Tor?"

Tor smiled and nodded. "Like it was yesterday," he said. "Sierra was an amazing chaser in his time. Maybe we should hang this in his stall so he can look at it and relive his glory days as a jumper."

"At twenty-four, he's earned his retirement," Ashleigh commented. "But I think he'd rather have an extra measure of grain than the photo."

"How about hanging it in the office instead?" Samantha suggested, prying a third box open. "More pictures," she announced, pulling a photo album from the box and flipping it open. "Look, Cindy. Here's one of you with Max Smith and Glory."

Cindy glanced at the picture. "March to Glory," she said fondly, smiling at the photo of the gray stallion. "He's still an awesome horse."

"And one of the best stallions we have at Whitebrook," Christina said, peeking over Cindy's shoulder at the photo. "You look so young in this picture."

Cindy nodded. "I was barely eighteen. That was just before I left to go to Dubai." She sighed. "I was such an overly confident little brat back then."

"You were a tough, competitive jockey," Samantha countered. "You knew what you wanted and you went after it."

"And earned fame on the New York tracks as a top-notch jockey," Ashleigh pointed out. "We were all very proud of what you accomplished on your own, Cindy."

"I never would have been able to do it if it hadn't been for all of you," Cindy said. "I was so lucky to end up with such a wonderful family and good friends around me. I just didn't appreciate it for a long time." She smiled at Ashleigh and Samantha. "Everything I've accomplished I owe to you two and Dad." Cindy, orphaned as a youngster, had found a home at Whitebrook, where Samantha's father, Ian McLean, was the head trainer. Ian and Beth, Samantha's stepmother, had adopted Cindy, making her part of their extended family, along with Samantha and Cindy's younger brother, Kevin.

"Whatever happened to Max Smith?" Tor asked as he moved another box. "I thought you two were going to be the couple of the century, Cindy."

"He went to California to go to veterinary school about the same time I moved to Dubai with Champion," Cindy said. At eighteen, she had gone to the United Arab Emirates to take care of Wonder's Champion. The stallion, co-owned by Ashleigh and Clay Townsend, had been sold to Ben al-Rihani's father. Cindy had spent a year in Dubai before she returned to the United States to work in New York as a jockey. "I thought someday we'd end up back together, but life doesn't always work out the way we plan, does it?"

"That's for sure," Samantha said, pulling a pair of riding boots from the box in front of her. "These can go to the clothing bank. Some kid will be able to use them."

"Look at all this," Christina said, pulling old ribbons, rolled posters, and schedules from a box.

"Those are from when we were in charge of the Pony Commandos," Tor said. "I didn't realize we still had all that stuff."

"The riding program for handicapped kids?" Christina asked. "I see a lot of write-ups about it in the paper. It sounds like an awesome group."

"Tor helped set up the Pony Commandos when I

was still in high school," Samantha said. "We had some great kids in that club, didn't we, Tor?"

"You remember Mandy Jarvis, don't you?" Ashleigh asked.

"Of course," Samantha said. "She was one of the original kids, and now she's running the program. I keep in pretty close touch with her, since she has Shining."

"That was a deal that worked out great for both of you," Ashleigh said. "Mandy loves Shining as much as you do. I couldn't imagine a better home for the mare."

"I know," Samantha agreed. "Shining couldn't be any more content with Mandy and her husband, Phil."

"We should take this box of Pony Commandos memorabilia over to her," Tor said. "I'm sure she'd get a kick out of seeing some of this."

"That's a great idea," Samantha said.

"Can I go when you do?" Christina asked. "I barely remember Mandy. I'd like to see her again."

"We'll plan a visit on a day you don't have class," Samantha promised.

The group fell silent as they sorted through boxes, quickly clearing out a large part of the room.

"I'll put these boxes for the clothing bank in my car," Cindy said finally. "I can drop them off on my way home this afternoon."

"I'll help you carry them out," Tor volunteered.

"Oh, wait," Christina said as Cindy started to rise. "Here's another box full of clothes. This is probably stuff that can go, too." But her eyes widened as she pulled a tissue-wrapped garment from the box. "This looks like a wedding dress," she said, carefully unwrapping the gown.

"Oh!" Samantha clapped her hands to her face. "My wedding gown! I packed it away before we left for Ireland, and I'd forgotten where I put it."

Christina rose and gently smoothed the satin fabric of the creamy white floor-length dress, with its full, ruffle-covered skirt and fitted lacy bodice. "This is a beautiful gown, Sammy," she said.

"Hold it up to yourself," Samantha urged her. When Christina complied, Samantha smiled broadly. "You're not much taller than me," she said, then looked down at her stomach. "And I think I used to be about your weight."

"It looks like it would be a perfect fit for Chris," Cindy said.

"I think so, too," Samantha said thoughtfully. "How about it, Ashleigh?"

Christina's mother smiled. "I know she couldn't wear my old dress," she said. "It would be way too short for her."

"I'm not ready for a wedding dress!" Christina exclaimed. "I have years of college to get through. Besides, Parker and I haven't even discussed it." Christina's boyfriend, Parker Townsend, was in England, training with other members of the United States Equestrian Team under Jack Dalton, a well-known three-day eventing coach.

"Ooh," Cindy said. "Speaking of weddings and the Townsends, remember Brad and Lavinia's big to-do? The paper ran a two-page spread with photos of the celebrities who showed up for their ceremony. The social pages read like the who's who of the East Coast."

"I remember it," Ashleigh said, shaking her head. "I couldn't believe we were invited. That was probably the biggest shindig Kentucky has ever seen. Their party made Mike's and my wedding at Whitebrook seem pretty dull." Parker's parents, Brad and Lavinia, owned Townsend Acres, a large and highly successful Kentucky Thoroughbred farm. While Christina and Parker were close, there was no fondness between the Reese family and the Townsends. Over the years they had co-owned a number of Thoroughbred racehorses,

13

which had caused a lot of tension between the two families.

"You and Mike had a great wedding," Samantha countered. "It was so beautiful, and Whitebrook was the perfect setting for it."

"In spite of all the setbacks, you and Tor managed to have a pretty special celebration, too," Ashleigh replied, pointing at the dress. "I can still remember you in that dress. You made the most stunning couple I have ever seen, with your gorgeous long hair streaming down your back, and Tor in his dark suit." She smiled fondly.

"I was so little, I can barely remember it," Christina said, rewrapping the dress to set it aside. "But I do remember thinking that it was the most wonderful wedding in the world."

"I'll never forget it," Ashleigh said with a chuckle. "That was the wedding we thought was never going to happen."

"What do you mean?" Christina asked, looking curiously from Samantha to her mother.

"I think you need to take that dress home," Samantha said quickly. "It would mean a lot to me if you got married in my wedding dress." She glanced up at Tor and smiled fondly at him. "Maybe it would help ensure that you'll be as happy and Tor and I are."

"Don't change the subject," Christina said, wrinkling her nose at Samantha. "What did Mom mean, no one thought your wedding was ever going to happen?"

Samantha looked to Tor, and he smiled at her and nodded. "I think you should tell Christina the story," he said. "I'll help Cindy carry these boxes out to her car, and you can fill Christina in on how we almost didn't make it to the altar."

"I'll get the food," Ashleigh offered. "It's time for a break, anyway. We can have an indoor picnic right here on the floor." She rose as Tor and Cindy began picking up boxes.

Samantha leaned back against the wall and wrapped her hands around her knees. She closed her eyes for a moment and drifted back in time, thinking of the months before she and Tor married. "Looking back on it, the whole thing seems a lifetime ago," she said, slipping into a hint of the Irish brogue she had picked up from her years in Ireland. "But thinking about it now, sure, I can see it all as though the wedding were just yesterday." She looked up at Christina and smiled. "It wasn't an easy thing, making that wedding a reality," she said.

"So tell me about it," Christina urged, sitting in front of Samantha, a look of eager anticipation on her face.

"Well," Samantha said slowly, a smile spreading across her face, "it all began with another wedding."

2

"I CAN'T BELIEVE HOW NERVOUS I AM," TWENTY-THREE-year-old Samantha McLean said, looking around the vestibule of the church. Groups of well-dressed people were walking through the entry, where they were greeted by the waiting ushers.

"Are you with the bride's family or the groom's?" one of the young men asked the arriving guests before leading them to the proper side of the church.

What a wonderful way to start a life together, she thought, smiling at several people as they strolled into the church.

"I swear, half of Lexington is here for the wedding," Maureen O'Brien said. Samantha's friend from high school leaned to the side to peek through the wide double doors that led into the church, inspecting the crowded pews. "I just know I'm going to do something dumb like trip while we're walking down the aisle."

"Me too," Samantha said, nervously turning the bridesmaid bouquet she held, just to keep her hands busy. "I wish I'd worn flat shoes instead of these heels. I feel like a newborn foal trying to walk for the first time."

"You both need to relax." Beth McLean, Samantha's stepmother, slipped her arm around Samantha's waist and gave her a quick squeeze. "Everything is lovely, and you girls look beautiful in those dresses. This is going to be a very nice wedding."

"Thanks," Maureen said, smoothing the shimmering blue taffeta of her bridesmaid dress.

"I'm going to go sit down," Beth said, smiling at Samantha. "I left your father taking care of Kevin, and I'm sure your little brother isn't making it an easy job."

Samantha chuckled. At four years old, Kevin was a bundle of energy and curiosity, and she knew he wouldn't be too happy having to sit still and be quiet for very long. "Good luck," she told Beth.

As Beth walked away, Maureen heaved a sigh. "I know I should be really happy, but since we graduated from college, this is my third time being an attendant in someone else's wedding. I'm starting to think I'll always be a bridesmaid and never a bride."

Maureen had completed her degree in journalism a few months earlier and had just started working for the *Lexington Herald*. Samantha had been using her degree in business management to help Tor and his father run their stable at Whisperwood, where the Nelsons bred sport horses and taught show jumping.

Samantha laughed. "You're only twenty-three," she said. "I don't think that makes you an old maid."

"I know," Maureen said. "But when I see Yvonne and Gregg so happy, and you and Tor together, I wonder if I'll ever find someone who's just right for me."

"You will," Samantha reassured her friend. She lifted the bouquet of flowers to her face and inhaled the fragrance of the yellow rosebuds and pink-tinged orchids, then admired the combination of tiny blue forget-me-nots and delicate fronds of maidenhair fern that completed the arrangement.

Soft organ music drifted through the open doors, and Samantha peered around the corner as another group of people walked up the aisle. She could see Tor, tall, blond, and handsome in his tuxedo, standing next to Gregg Doherty and the minister at the front of the church. Gregg looked a little nervous, which made Samantha smile. She wondered if Tor would be anxious on their wedding day. Seeing him standing at the altar made her heart flutter a bit, and she stepped back from the doorway to wait for the organist to break into the wedding march.

"How do I look?" Yvonne Ortez asked, walking across the vestibule to where Samantha and Maureen were waiting, the full skirt of her cream-colored dress rustling as she walked. "Did I mess my hair up too much when I put the dress on?"

"You look beautiful," Maureen said quickly.

Samantha looked at her best friend and nodded in agreement. "Absolutely perfect," she said sincerely, admiring Yvonne's shiny dark hair, which had been smoothed back into a chignon and decorated with yellow rosebuds and forget-me-nots. Yvonne, with her English, Spanish, and Navajo heritage, looked fantastic. Samantha reached up to pat her own head of wavy red-brown hair. "I had to put so much styling gel in my hair to get it to stay in place that it feels like cement."

"Me too," Maureen said.

The music from inside the church increased in volume, and the three girls looked at each other as the organist broke into the traditional march. "It's time,"

Samantha said, feeling her pulse pick up, and she moved into her place in the procession.

The walk from the back of the church to the altar seemed to take an eternity, and Samantha forced herself to step slowly, trying to enjoy the significance of the stately march to the front of the church. She darted a quick look at Yvonne and saw her friend's attention fixed on the people at the altar. When Samantha looked back toward the front of the church, she saw Gregg gazing at Yvonne with absolute devotion. *They are going to be a very happy couple,* Samantha thought. *Just like Tor and me.*

When she looked from Gregg to Tor, his lips curved into a tiny smile, and he gave her a little wink. Samantha felt her tension melt a bit, and she smiled back. How did Tor manage to look so calm and relaxed, while she was a bundle of nerves?

Even when he was in the middle of a fast-paced steeplechase, he always looked like he was having the time of his life. After seeing photos of herself racing, Samantha knew that her expression conveyed the tension and determined concentration that she felt. Tor had better control than she did, she decided. She would have to take the time to figure out how she could do better, and she knew Tor would be there to help her.

What's there to be tense about now? she asked herself as they neared the altar. *This is going to be the most perfect wedding ever. I just know it. We're almost there, and I haven't done anything embarrassing. I'm going to make it to the front of the church without tripping over my dress or spraining my ankle.* She took a deep breath, feeling the tense knot in her stomach fade.

As the group mounted the steps to where the minister waited, solemn and dignified in his dark suit, Samantha caught Tor's eye again. The look on his face made her feel warm, and the words *I love you, Tor Nelson* sounded so loud in her head that she wondered for a moment if she had spoken them out loud.

Samantha moved to her place on the altar, gazing out over the crowded church while she waited for the minister to begin reading the vows. As he welcomed the wedding guests, Samantha spotted her father, Ian McLean, sitting with Beth. Kevin was wedged in between them, his red hair tousled and dirt on the white shirt Beth had made him wear. Samantha smiled to herself. She could tell Kevin thought he was being tortured unbearably, with his arms folded in front of him and a scowl on his face.

Samantha's sister, Cindy, was sitting next to them. She leaned over and whispered to her boyfriend, Max

Smith, who was seated beside her, and Max nodded at whatever comment Cindy made. Petite, blond-haired Cindy looked bored. Samantha knew her sister would rather be in the barn with the racehorses than sitting in the church. At seventeen, Cindy was already an accomplished jockey. She planned to leave Kentucky for New York as soon as she graduated from high school and make her living jockeying the Thoroughbreds she loved.

Beside Ian and Beth, Ashleigh Griffen and Mike Reese were sitting together. Christina was sitting on Mike's lap, playing with the buttons on her father's dress shirt. Samantha smiled to herself. At four, Christina was already a dedicated equestrienne, riding her pony, a brown-and-white paint nicknamed Trib, every day. Even though her parents trained racehorses, Christina seemed more interested in jumping, a passion she shared with Samantha and Tor.

Scattered throughout the church, Samantha saw several of her high school classmates, and most of the members of the Pony Commandos and their families. Dark-skinned, curly-haired Mandy Jarvis was sitting between her parents, a dreamy look on her face as she gazed up at the altar. At thirteen, Mandy had an incredible romantic streak, and she had volunteered a lot of input into planning the wedding. The yellow roses in the bouquets that decorated the church had been her idea. "Roses for love, and yellow for best friends forever," she had said. "You should be best friends with the person you marry."

Samantha agreed wholeheartedly, thinking of Tor. They shared a lot of interests in common, the main thing being their passion for horses, and Samantha would rather spend time with Tor than anyone else.

"Maybe you should become a wedding consultant when you grow up," Samantha had teased Mandy. "You sure have a lot of good ideas."

Mandy had shaken her head. "I'm going to do something with horses," she'd said stubbornly. "Working on horseback has gotten me to the point where I don't have to wear those horrible leg braces anymore, and I want to help other kids."

"Good for you," Samantha had said, pleased with Mandy's plan for the future. Injured in an accident when she was six, Mandy had struggled to regain the use of her legs, and therapeutic riding had played an important role in her recovery.

As the minister concluded a brief prayer, Samantha's attention snapped back to the present. How could she let her mind wander at a time like this?

"We are gathered here," the minister said, "to witness the marriage of two wonderful young people. I am honored to perform this wedding ceremony for Gregg Doherty and Yvonne Ortez."

Samantha glanced at Yvonne, who looked radiant as she stood beside Gregg, her frothy wedding dress sweeping the floor. With his black tuxedo and neatly trimmed hair, gazing down at Yvonne with an adoring look, Gregg made Samantha think of the little groom figurine on a wedding cake. *They're going to be together forever,* Samantha told herself, sighing happily.

The minister read the vows that Gregg and Yvonne had written for each other, and Samantha let the promises of love and devotion wash over her. Soon Tor was handing Gregg the bride's ring, and Samantha gave Yvonne the groom's ring, giving her friend's hand a soft squeeze as she passed her the band.

"I now pronounce you husband and wife," the minister announced. As the newlyweds kissed, the crowded church resounded with organ music again, and Samantha fell in beside Tor to follow Gregg and Yvonne out of the church.

"That was a beautiful wedding." Samantha sighed when they got outside.

Tor nodded, taking Samantha by the arm and guiding her toward the reception hall, where caterers had laid out a long table covered with food. At the center of the table sat the multitiered wedding cake, decorated with yellow sugar roses. The wedding gifts were stacked on a smaller table, and Samantha saw the gift she and Tor had selected for their friends. Inside the silver-wrapped box was a soft throw that had Gregg and Yvonne's names and wedding date woven into the pattern.

After standing in the reception line for several minutes, Samantha found a spot by the refreshment table, and as the band began to play, she watched Gregg and Yvonne whirl around the room to an old-fashioned waltz.

"They look so happy," she murmured to Tor, who slipped his arm around her waist and pulled her close to his side.

"They make a good couple," Tor agreed, then glanced down at Samantha. "Just like you and me."

"Doesn't this make the two of you think about setting a date for your wedding?" Ashleigh Griffin asked, pouring punch into a cup.

Samantha gave Ashleigh a startled look. "We aren't even engaged," she said.

"Actually, I was thinking maybe it's time to change that," Tor said, reaching into his pocket. He produced a small box and opened it, holding it out for Samantha to see. "See, it took me forever to find the right ring for you," he said.

She stared at the ring. It was covered with several small diamonds that sat within the gold band, leaving a smooth surface. She looked up at him and smiled. "Oh, Tor," she said in a quiet voice, pressing her hand to her mouth. "It's beautiful."

"If you don't like it, we can take it back," he said quickly. "If you want to pick out something different, that's okay with me."

Samantha looked from the ring to Tor's anxious expression and shook her head. "I love it," she told him. "It's perfect." The stones glittered inside the smooth setting, catching the light.

"I would like to have given you a huge diamond, but it didn't seem practical. I didn't want you to worry about catching the ring on something and damaging it, so this made the most sense to me." He gave Samantha another worried look. "That doesn't sound very romantic, does it?"

"It's perfect," she said, running her finger along the row of diamonds. Of course Tor would know she wouldn't want something that might get damaged while she was working in the barn. "You picked the exact ring I would have," she said. "You knew what I wanted."

Tor lifted it from the box and smiled down at her. "Then you'll wear it, Sammy? You'll marry me?"

Samantha gazed into his eyes and nodded silently, not trusting herself to speak. When Tor took her hand and slipped the ring onto her finger, she released a shaky sigh.

"This is just wonderful," Ashleigh said, coming around the table to give them both a hug. "I am so happy for you two."

Yvonne and Gregg came off the floor as their dance ended, and guests began to dance as the band struck up a new song.

"What's this?" Yvonne asked, her eyes lighting up when she saw the ring on Samantha's finger. "It's about time!" she exclaimed, clapping her hands together. "I think now is a good time to make the announcement, don't you?"

"But this is your special day," Samantha protested. "You need to cut the cake, make toasts, and be the center of attention."

"Then you can announce it after the toasts," Gregg said, clapping his hand on Tor's shoulder.

"Congratulations, buddy. I wish you both all the happiness in the world."

Tor looked at Samantha and smiled. "I think I found it."

When the guests had gathered close for the cutting of the wedding cake, Ashleigh tapped Samantha's shoulder. "I'm going to get your parents," she said, hurrying off to where Mr. Nelson was standing with Ian and Beth.

After the cake had been cut and various people had proposed toasts to the newlyweds, Tor and Samantha shared the news of their engagement, and the crowd in the hall broke into applause.

Mandy hurried over to them, her eyes sparkling with delight. "Another wedding," she said excitedly. "This is going to be so great."

"Will you be one of my bridesmaids?" Samantha asked the girl.

Mandy's expression fell a little, and she shook her head. "You don't want me limping down the aisle," she said with a frown. "It would spoil the whole thing."

Samantha wrapped her arms around Mandy. "Not having you as part of the wedding would spoil it," she countered.

Tor rested his hand on Mandy's thin shoulder.

"I'll give you a piggyback ride down the aisle if that's the only way you'll be in the wedding," he offered, giving her a wink.

Mandy laughed and nodded. "I'll do it," she said, smiling at Tor. "I'll work hard to get rid of my limp before the wedding, so you don't have to carry me down the aisle."

When the band started to play a slow song, Tor took Samantha by the hand and led her to the floor. Gregg and Yvonne followed them, and the rest of the afternoon passed in a happy blur for Samantha.

As the reception began to wind down, Yvonne pulled Samantha aside. "We have to leave," Yvonne said. "We don't want to miss our flight to Italy."

"An Italian honeymoon," Samantha said. "That's going to be so romantic."

Yvonne nodded. "And you're next," she said, her eyes sparkling. "Don't make any plans until Gregg and I get back. I want to help you." Yvonne held out her bride's bouquet, pressing the flowers into Samantha's hands. "I want you to have this," she said.

"But you're supposed to toss it into the crowd," Samantha protested. "Whoever catches it is supposed to be the next one to get married."

Yvonne shrugged and grinned. "It's my wedding

and I'll do what I want," she said saucily. "You're going to be the next one to get married, and that's that." She gestured at the floral bouquets that filled the hall. "Can you make sure all the other flowers go to the nursing home?" she asked. "They're so lovely, I want to share them, and obviously I'm not taking them to Italy."

"I'll take care of it," Samantha promised.

Gregg walked up to them, his jacket draped over his shoulder, and wrapped his arm around Yvonne's waist. "Are you ready to go, Mrs. Doherty?" he asked.

Yvonne looked up at him and nodded, then leaned over to plant a quick kiss on Samantha's cheek. "Remember," she whispered. "When I get back, we have a wedding to plan."

She took Gregg's hand, and they made their way to the sidewalk, laughing as the crowd in front of the hall showered them with rice. As they climbed into the waiting limousine, Samantha stood in the doorway of the reception hall and watched them go. She held the bridal bouquet close and wiggled her ring finger, thinking of how wonderful and how strange it was to be wearing an engagement ring.

I get to plan Tor's and my wedding, she told herself.

The thought seemed almost dreamlike, and Samantha sighed happily.

I can hardly wait, she thought. I want to have the
most perfect wedding ever, something we'll remember for
the rest of our lives.

3

"LET ME SEE THE RING AGAIN," MANDY SAID, LEANING over Butterball's shoulder to look at Samantha's hand. Samantha was standing in the middle of the indoor arena at Whisperwood, watching Mandy work with her pony, while Tor was preparing some of the other small horses for the riding class, scheduled to start in a few minutes.

A month had passed since Yvonne and Gregg's wedding. Samantha had gotten a postcard from Italy, telling her that they were extending their vacation. Samantha was glad her friends were having such a wonderful time, but she wished Yvonne would hurry back to help her make some of her own wedding plans.

"You've only looked at the ring a dozen times in the last hour," Samantha teased Mandy.

"I know," Mandy said, grinning. "But show me again." Samantha agreeably raised her left hand and let Mandy admire the engagement ring.

"I think you need to wear a beaded white satin wedding dress with a lace train that sweeps the floor," Mandy said. "And white roses everywhere, tons of them. It'll be an exquisite wedding."

"Exquisite?" Samantha grinned at Mandy. "You do like to plan big, don't you?"

"You're only getting married once, and I know exactly how things should look," Mandy replied.

Samantha patted Butterball's tan shoulder and stepped back. "We have plenty of time to figure it out," she said, wanting to get Mandy off the subject of an ornate ceremony. "Let's see you ride."

"Okay," Mandy said, cueing Butterball into a walk. Tor strode across the arena and put his arm over Samantha's shoulder. "Mandy's getting too big for that pony," he commented, watching her move Butterball into a bouncy trot. "Sit deeper in the saddle," he called automatically as Mandy jostled a bit to Butterball's short strides. Mandy straightened up and corrected her seat, then flashed a quick grin over her shoulder at Tor.

"It's a good thing she isn't a tall girl," Samantha commented. "Butterball's been just right for her for a long time, but she really does need a full-size horse."

"To look at her, you'd never know that she was hobbling around in leg braces until just a couple of years ago," Tor said.

"Have Mr. and Mrs. Jarvis talked to you about a horse for Mandy?" Samantha asked, leaning against Tor's side.

He nodded. "It has to be just the right one," he said. "Mandy's special, and she needs a special horse."

"I'm sure you'll find the perfect animal," Samantha said. She smiled up at Tor. "You seem to do everything just right." She wiggled her ring finger and eyed the sparkling diamonds that studded the gold band. "Like this."

Tor glanced down at the ring, then at Samantha. "We still need to figure out a date," he said.

"That's going to take some doing," Samantha said with a little sigh. "We've got a show to put together for the Pony Commandos, the Bright Meadows Chase for Charity next month, and the big steeplechase at Kentucky Horse Park coming up. If we wait too long, Shining will be ready to foal, and I'd hate to try to plan a wedding around her due date."

Tor nodded. "We'll manage. But you're right, we have a lot going on." He got a thoughtful look on his face. "It would be great to get the big High Hopes Steeplechase at the Kentucky Horse Park to contribute a share of the money they raise for disabled riding programs to the Pony Commandos. Without more help, we can't expand the program beyond what it is now."

"We've pushed it to the limit as it is," Samantha agreed. "I've been going through the accounts, and even with the volunteer help and donations we get, the Commandos are still costing you out of your own pocket."

Tor shrugged. "I know," he said. "But every penny I spend is worth it."

Samantha looked at him, a warm feeling spreading through her. "And your caring so much about the kids is one of the many things I love about you," she said. "Speaking of which, we need to get to work. Beth and Janet will be here any minute with the kids."

Some of the riders that Beth McLean and Janet Roarsh brought in had been with the Commandos since the beginning, while others, like Mandy, had made such gains through the riding program that they no longer needed help. But Timmy Alonso and Robert Simon, at thirteen, were still wheelchair-bound, as were some of the other, younger students whose parents and assistants brought them to the class.

Beth pushed Timmy's wheelchair up the ramp that led to the special platform Tor and his father had built so that the kids who need help mounting could easily get onto their horses' backs. The rest of the riders lined up, and volunteers helped the students mount up.

"I miss having Yvonne and Gregg here to help," Samantha told Tor as she took Zorro's lead line, then wrinkled her nose and grinned at him mischievously. "They'd better be having a wonderful time in Venice."

"I'm sure they are," Tor said, patting the black pony's graying muzzle. He smiled at the little girl sitting on his back. "Are you ready to go, Lisa?"

The six-year-old nodded, a serious expression on her round face. "I'm using my legs just like you told me to," she informed them. "And I'm sitting straight as a stick."

"You're doing a great job," Tor replied.

For several minutes the adults led the young riders around the arena, letting the rhythm of the walking ponies encourage the riders to use their muscles to maintain balance and build strength. After a long warm-up, some of the students were allowed to ride on their own, with an adult coaching each of them as they walked and jogged their mounts around the arena.

When the class was over, Cory Jones, an eight-year-old with Down syndrome, wrapped his arms around his pony's neck, burying his face in Lollipop's dappled gray coat. He inhaled deeply, then grinned up at Samantha. "I'm remembering what he smells like until next week," he said, giving the gentle pony a kiss on the nose. As his mother led him from the arena, Cory kept turning to wave good-bye to Lollypop. Samantha smiled to herself as she watched him go. It was so great to work with the animals she loved, and with people who cared about horses as much as she did. *I'm very lucky*, she told herself, watching Tor wave to several students who were leaving the stable.

Tor began untacking the ponies while Samantha started putting the arena equipment away. When she met him in the tack room, his arms were loaded with bridles.

"We still have a little time this afternoon," he said as Samantha began hanging up the bridles. "If you don't mind, I'd like to get Sierra out and see how he looks under saddle. We need to start getting him geared up for the Chase for Charity."

"I'm glad Mike agreed to let him stay here," Samantha said. "It gives me more chances to work with him." Since Mike and Ashleigh worked only with flat-track racers, Sierra had been moved to Whisperwood, where Tor and Samantha had continued his training as a jumper, a sport Sierra excelled at.

"I think it is so cool that Bright Meadows has offered to host a special day to raise money for the Pony Commandos," Samantha added. "I'll get Sierra's tack if you'll get him out."

In a few minutes they had the big Thoroughbred, a handsome liver chestnut, in the cross ties. Samantha quickly groomed Sierra while Tor went out to move some of the jumps that were set up in the outdoor arena.

"It's all ready," he announced, coming back into the barn as Samantha was tightening Sierra's girth.

With Tor's help, Samantha had become an accomplished steeplechaser, winning several races on the local courses, always astride Sierra. Even though her heart was in her throat during every race, Samantha loved the intensity of racing over the fences. She trusted Sierra, who had a knack for reading the course, knowing when to rate himself for the jumps and when to run at top speed on the flat.

39

She led Sierra to the arena, and Tor gave her a leg up onto the saddle. "Easy," Samantha said, patting the big Thoroughbred's dark brown neck. The nine-year-old jumper snorted and pranced, tugging against the hold Samantha had on his reins. She smiled down at Tor. "He still acts like a colt," she said.

Tor nodded. "He's in excellent condition," he agreed. "Let's see what the two of you can do over those obstacles."

Samantha rode Sierra into the arena, warming him up before she moved the eager horse into a canter, circling the outer edge of the jumps Tor had set up. When she headed him for the first of the four-foot brush jumps, Sierra angled his head a little, measuring the jump as they approached it. She smiled to herself. "Even after all the training Tor has given me, I'm still just a passenger for you," she told the horse, moving into jumping position. "You're the old pro here. I have a lot more to learn about steeplechasing." Sierra cleared the jump easily, and Samantha turned him toward the next fence, pulling him in a little to shorten his strides so that he could take off the right distance from the jump. After they had completed the round, she rode back to Tor, who was waiting by the fence.

"He looks excellent," he announced. "I'm looking

forward to the Bright Meadows chase. It'll be a good warm-up for him before the High Hopes race. You two will be great."

"He is awesome," Samantha said, hopping from Sierra's back. She ran her hand along his shoulder. "He's barely warm," she said. "It won't take long to cool him out."

Tor pulled the saddle from Sierra's back while Samantha slipped his halter on, and when she began walking the horse, Tor hung the saddle on the fence and fell into step beside her. "So, about those wedding plans," he said. "We really should set a date, you know. You tell me when, and I'll help every way I can." He paused as they passed the turnout where Top Hat, Tor's white Thoroughbred jumper, was grazing. The horse lifted his head and nickered, walking to the fence so that Tor could pet him.

"Have you picked up any of those bride's magazines to look at?" he asked Samantha as Top Hat went back to grazing.

Samantha laughed, leading Sierra along the tractor trail between the paddocks. "I hadn't even thought about it," she admitted. "But if you can find the time to pick some up, I'd love to sit down with you and go through them."

Tor rolled his eyes. "I get the point," he said.

Samantha nodded. "We've both been a little busy."

"That's an understatement," Tor replied. "You've been doing so much to help Dad and me, and working with the racehorses at Whitebrook, and with the Brightons to organize the Chase for Charity event, and taking care of things for the Pony Commandos. Then there was Yvonne and Gregg's wedding, and—"

"Stop!" Samantha exclaimed. "It doesn't seem like I'm doing a lot, but when you start listing things, it makes me tired just to hear it all. Besides," she added, "I'm not the only one who's been overloaded. You haven't exactly been slacking."

"Okay," Tor said. "We're both doing a lot."

"But while we're on the subject, there is one thing I'd really like to do," Samantha said, tugging at Sierra's lead as he paused to nip at a patch of grass. "What would you think about a honeymoon in the Caribbean? The pictures Ashleigh and Mike brought back after their wedding trip made me think it must be the most beautiful place in the world."

"I like the idea," Tor said. "I've been putting money away so we can have a great honeymoon."

"I have, too," Samantha said. "We should be able to really enjoy ourselves."

"Well, now that we've got that settled, I guess we

need to cover some other things," Tor said. "I'm going to ask Mike to be my best man."

"Perfect," Samantha said. "I'm asking Ashleigh to be my matron of honor, and Christina and Kevin will be the ring bearer and flower girl. Cindy, Yvonne, Mandy, and Maureen will be the bridesmaids."

Sierra snorted loudly, drawing their attention back to him. Tor ran his hand along the horse's muscular chest. "He's cooled off," he said, and they led Sierra back toward the barn. Tor grabbed the saddle from the fence while Samantha took Sierra inside and clipped him to the cross ties. In the distance she heard the stable phone ringing.

"Sammy," she heard Mr. Nelson call from doorway of the barn. "You need to call Beth at her office. She says she has some good news for you."

"I'll groom Sierra if you want to make that call," Tor said.

"I'll be back to help you," Samantha promised.

Mr. Nelson was seated at his desk when Samantha walked into the office. He gave her a warm smile and started to rise, indicating that she should take his chair.

"That's okay," Samantha said quickly. "I don't want to bother you. I'm sure I won't be on the phone long."

She sat in the visitor's chair, and Mr. Nelson pushed the phone across the desk where she could reach it. "Take your time," he said. "You're never a bother, Samantha."

She dialed Beth's work number, and Beth answered on the first ring. "I have the country club scheduled for the wedding," she said excitedly. "It's going to be lovely, Sammy."

Samantha bit at her lower lip, not sure that she liked the idea of having her wedding at the exclusive country club. But Beth sounded so pleased about the arrangements she had made that Samantha couldn't say no.

"That's wonderful," Samantha said, struggling with her mixed feelings. "Thanks so much, Beth."

"The only problem," Beth added, "is that if we don't take the hall when it's available, we'll have to wait almost six more months before we can book it again. Which means the wedding will happen soon, if that's all right with you."

"How soon?" Samantha asked cautiously.

"Early December," Beth said. "I know it doesn't seem like it gives you much time, but with all the people who want to help, I'm sure we can get it organized."

"Wow," Samantha said slowly. It all seemed too

soon, but she thought about how pleased Beth sounded. "That's perfect, Beth. I'm sure Tor will be fine with a winter wedding. It'll be great."

When she got off the phone, Mr. Nelson was gazing across the desk at her. "So I only have to wait a few months for my new daughter-in-law?" he asked with a twinkle in his eye.

"Tor may not want to get married that quickly," Samantha said. "I guess I need to talk to him about having the wedding at the country club."

"If he has any complaints, send him in here," Mr. Nelson said, a mock frown on his face. "We'll have a little chat and I'll get him straightened right out."

Samantha chuckled. "I'm sure you would," she said, then paused, suddenly uncertain of what to call her future father-in-law. She didn't feel right calling him by his first name, but saying "Mr. Nelson" seemed a little too formal now that she and Tor were engaged.

"You know, Sammy," he said, leaning forward and resting his forearms on the desk, "if I had to pick the person I would want for a daughter-in-law, you would be my first choice. I am so happy that Tor finally put that ring on your finger."

Samantha smiled at him. "I am, too," she said.

"I hope now that we're going to be family, you'll

think of me as your second father," he said. "In fact, it would mean a lot to me if you would just call me Dad. You don't have to wait for the wedding."

Samantha felt a rush of fondness for Tor's father, and she nodded. "Thank you," she said, coming around the desk to give him a quick hug. "That's just how I think of you, as my other dad."

"Good," he said. "Now you'd better get out there and inform my son that the wedding date has been set. And I," he said with a grin, "need to call and reserve a tuxedo for the occasion. If there's anything I can do to help, just let me know."

"I will," Samantha promised, heading for the door.

Sierra was already back in his turnout, and Tor was moving the jumps in the outdoor arena when Samantha came outside.

"You look a little dazed," Tor commented as she nudged her toe against a cavalletti pole, moving it a few inches.

"I am," she said, looking up at him. "Beth booked the country club for our wedding. In December."

"And that isn't what you had in mind," Tor observed.

Samantha shook her head slowly. "I thought something a little simpler would be just fine," she said. "And I never thought about how soon. But everyone seems to think we need something extraordinary."

"Our wedding should be exceptional," Tor said. "But if you want something different, just say so."

"Well," Samantha said slowly, "I guess I really don't care when or where we get married." She gazed up at Tor. "I just want to spend the rest of my life with you."

"Me too," Tor said, wrapping his arms around her. "And really, Sammy, things could be much worse than having the wedding at the club."

"You're right," Samantha said. "Beth is excited about it, and I'm sure it will work out just fine." She smiled and tilted her head back to give Tor a soft kiss. "I'm happy. In fact," she said, "I'm so happy I think I could just burst."

"Oh, no! Don't do that," Tor said quickly. "I don't want to have to clean all that happiness off the arena footing."

"Very funny," Samantha said, adjusting another one of the cavalletti poles so that the spacing between the rails was right for the horses to work over.

"We'll have to rush in order to get everything ready," Tor said, setting a rail in place for a three-foot jump.

"I know," Samantha said. She glanced at her watch. "I'd better scoot," she said. "I promised Dad I'd be at Whitebrook half an hour ago to help with the yearlings."

"I'll talk to you later," Tor said, returning Samantha's quick good-bye kiss.

Samantha hurried to her car as Tor continued to arrange the arena for the next day's class.

When she reached Whitebrook, Samantha parked at the training barn and walked inside. Vic Taleski, the head groom, was leading a leggy chestnut filly up the aisle. "How's it going?" he greeted Samantha, stopping so she could pet the filly, a daughter of March to Glory and Townsend Princess. Princess, out of Ashleigh's Wonder, was one of the horses Ashleigh co-owned with the Townsends, who shared ownership of Wonder and all her offspring. While Clay Townsend had been incredibly generous when he gave Ashleigh a half interest in Wonder, trying to work with his son and daughter-in-law made life at Whitebrook a little stressful at times.

"Great, Vic," she said, admiring the filly. "Things couldn't be any better."

The groom grinned at her. "You do have a glow about you," he said. "I'm really happy for you and Tor, Sammy." He paused, then took a deep breath. "I know it's pretty forward to ask, but I do hope I'm invited to the wedding."

Samantha gave the groom a surprised look. "Of course," she said. "You're at the top of the list, Vic. You and Len have to be there, along with everyone else involved with Whitebrook. You're all part of my family."

Vic smiled. "I wouldn't miss it for the world." He gave the filly's lead a gentle tug. "I'd better get her out to the paddock," he said. "Your dad has work for this little girl."

"I'd better grab a helmet and get out there, too," Samantha said. "I think he has work for me as well."

She hurried to the tack room as Vic led the filly away. Until Vic had mentioned being invited to the wedding, she hadn't given it that much thought. But now that it was on her mind, the list of things she needed to do seemed overwhelming. She had to think about guest lists and invitations, a dress, flowers, a cake, decorations. . . . She gave her head a quick shake and grabbed a helmet. How was she going to get everything organized and keep from losing her mind?

"HERE YOU GO, SHINING," SAMANTHA SAID, POURING A measure of grain into the chestnut mare's feed pan. It had been almost two weeks since Beth had booked the country club, but Samantha hadn't had time to do any planning for the wedding. Although she had started to enjoy the idea of a fabulous, memorable ceremony, the pressure she felt about all the organizing took away some of the fun.

She set the grain measure in the wheelbarrow with the other empty cans. Samantha had given the rest of the mares their morning feed, saving Shining's for last so that she could spend a little time with her horse before she finished her chores.

"I don't know where to begin with all this wedding stuff," she told Shining. "It must be nice to be a horse. You don't have a lot of worries, do you, girl?"

Shining eyed the pan of grain, then gave Samantha a nudge with her long nose.

"What is it?" Samantha asked, running her hand along Shining's glossy neck. "You want pickles and ice cream, don't you?"

She eyed the mare's round side, then leaned over the stall door and rattled the grain pan. "Now eat up." Shining snorted softly, then dropped her nose in the pan and began nibbling the feed.

"Good girl," Samantha said. "You still have months to go before this foal is born. You need all those vitamins and minerals, whether you like the taste or not."

Shining, half sister to Ashleigh's prized Thoroughbred mare, Ashleigh's Wonder, was the first horse Samantha had ever owned. When Mike had rescued Shining as a badly neglected three-year-old, Samantha had nursed the filly back to health, making a winning racehorse out of her. To repay Samantha for her hard work and dedication, Mike and Ashleigh had given Samantha the roan mare.

Now, at nine, Shining had produced several exceptional foals, sired by Blues King, Jazzman, and March to Glory, some of Whitebrook's best stallions.

Samantha had kept Shining's first filly, Lucky Chance, sired by Chance Remark. Though she would have rather kept every one of Shining's foals, she had made the decision to sell the mare's other colts and fillies to pay for her education.

Now Shining was in foal again to Jazzman, and Samantha was dreaming of the beautiful Thoroughbred foal the mare would give her early next year. "I finally get to keep another one of your babies," she told the mare. "Isn't that going to be wonderful? It's time Tor and I got serious about building up our stock for our own farm." Shining snorted softly, nudging the grain around in the feed pan.

"Eat," Samantha urged her. "You need to stay strong and healthy."

"Hey, Sammy!"

Samantha looked down the barn aisle to see Maureen O'Brien standing near the office, holding a stack of magazines. "Hi, Maureen," she said, waving to her friend. "What are you doing here at this time of the morning?" Maureen put in long hours of work at the *Herald*, which meant she didn't have a lot of time to spend with her friends anymore. Samantha's own hectic schedule kept her from being able to visit much, too, so she was happy to see her friend at the barn.

"I'm on my way to work," Maureen said, glancing at her watch as she strolled down the aisle toward Samantha. She paused at Precocious's stall to pat the mare's sleek black nose, then stopped to give Wonder a pat, and then again at Townsend Princess's stall. When she reached Samantha and Shining, she smiled at the mare, who continued to eat slowly. "She doesn't look too pregnant to me," Maureen said, stroking Shining's poll.

"When you already weigh a thousand pounds it takes a while to start showing," Samantha said with a laugh.

"I stopped by because I thought you might want these," Maureen said, indicating the bundle she held. "I collected the bridal magazines and catalogs from the other girls whose weddings I was in. I'm sure they'll give you some great ideas."

Samantha took one of the thick books from Maureen and flipped through it, stopping at a page that showed a model in an intricately decorated gown. The fitted bodice of the dress was covered with silk embroidery, while the skirt swept the ground in layers of shimmering fabric. The model was wearing elbow-length white gloves and a diamond necklace, and an elegant tiara rested on top of her carefully styled hair.

"Oh, no," Samantha said in dismay. "I can't imagine wearing something like that." Her idea of the perfect wedding gown was much simpler, something far less grand than the dress in the magazine.

"But you'd look beautiful in that," Maureen protested. "You're only getting married once. You need to go all out with everything!" She flipped open one of the other magazines and held up a picture of white orchids, white roses, and silver ribbons combined in a stunning bouquet. "How about flowers like this?"

"That is beautiful," Samantha agreed, gazing at the arrangement. She imagined herself walking down the aisle in the dress and tiara, the bouquet in her hands, stately organ music in the background, and she nodded. "That would be pretty cool," she agreed, looking at the floral design again.

Shining stuck her head over the top of her stall and snorted loudly, making Samantha laugh. "Shining would prefer a bouquet of good hay and carrot roses," she said, patting the mare's neck.

Maureen raised her eyebrows and shook her head. "I don't think they'll let you in the country club for the wedding, sweetheart," she told the horse.

"Wouldn't that be the scandal of the decade," Samantha said, wrinkling her nose. She grinned at

Maureen. "We could serve apple cake and fresh corn. The horses would love it, don't you think?"

"You need to get serious about this wedding thing," Maureen said sternly. "You don't have a lot of time, and you have tons of stuff to do."

Samantha sighed and leaned against the stall. "It's kind of overwhelming," she said. "I started making lists of what I need to get done, but it just boggles my mind. Besides, I have so many things to do at Whisperwood and here that I don't know how I'm going to find time to put the wedding together."

"These should help you," Maureen said, nodding at the magazines. "Right now I need to get to work." She sighed. "I never thought being the assistant to the managing editor at the paper would be so involved."

"I'm glad you brought the magazines," Samantha said. "Maybe they'll get me motivated."

"I'll leave them on the desk in the office so you can look through them," Maureen told her. "I'll see you later."

"Thanks for thinking of me," Samantha said, taking the handles of the wheelbarrow as Maureen left the barn.

When Samantha finally returned to the cottage late in the morning, the wedding magazines forgotten in the barn office, a strange car was parked by the door. She gave the expensive-looking sedan a curious look, then strode to the house, wondering who the visitor was.

Beth greeted her at the kitchen door. "I hope you don't mind, but since I know you're so busy, and time is getting short, I took it upon myself to hire a wedding planner."

"A wedding planner?" Samantha repeated, not sure if she should be relieved or concerned that other people were taking charge of planning her wedding. "How did you find someone to do that?"

Beth grinned sheepishly. "I talked to the woman who does most of the wedding parties at the country club," she confessed. "Your father and I want you to have everything just right, and I want to do whatever I can to make this a special day for you. Erika Alfonso has a great reputation for pulling together a spectacular celebration, so we agreed to hire her."

Samantha sucked in a surprised breath. "Isn't she the one who did Brad and Lavinia's wedding? I'm afraid she might be a little too upscale for the kind of wedding I'm picturing."

"I think she'll do a great job," Beth said as Samantha walked inside. "I never had a daughter to plan a wedding for, and I'm looking forward to seeing you and Tor have the best wedding ever."

Samantha relaxed a little and smiled agreeably. Beth wanted her to be happy, and Samantha was grateful to have a stepmother who cared so much. "Thanks, Beth," she said, giving the older woman a hug. "You really are the best."

"Come and meet Erika," Beth said. "We were just going through pictures of some of the weddings she's organized, and she has some great ideas."

"How did you get her to come over so quickly?" Samantha asked. "She probably has a waiting list of clients."

Beth nodded. "Erika takes aerobics classes from me, so I guess that helped. She had a free morning, and with the short time we have to get this organized, she wanted to get started."

Samantha sighed, trying to imagine the same woman who had put together Brad and Lavinia's huge, showy wedding organizing her far less extravagant one. But she had to agree, she didn't have the time or the experience to plan a wedding. Beth was going to make sure everything was taken care of.

She followed Beth into the living room, where a slender woman in a beige linen suit was sitting on the sofa. Erika Alfonso's short blond hair was carefully styled, and her makeup was perfectly done. She sat with her ankles crossed primly, her back straight, a cup of tea in her hand.

As Samantha took in the neatly manicured nails with polish that matched Erika's outfit, she cringed inwardly, thinking of her own stubby, unpainted nails and disheveled hair. She felt suddenly self-conscious in her jeans and paddock boots.

The McLeans' cottage was nicely decorated, thanks to Beth's care and good taste, but Erika's presence made the room seem shabby. But, Samantha reminded herself, this was her home, and she was proud of what Beth had done to decorate it. She smiled at Erika, not sure whether she should extend her hand. She doubted Erika Alfonso would appreciate the tiniest molecule of barn dirt anywhere near her.

"Do have a seat," Erika said, smiling at Samantha as she patted the space next to her on the sofa. "Beth has told me so much about you that I feel like I already know you, Samantha. I'm quite delighted to be able to help you plan your wedding."

Samantha sat down and clasped her hands together, surprised at how nervous she felt in Erika's company.

Erika glanced at the ring on Samantha's finger. "That is the most adorable little ring I have ever seen," she said.

Samantha stiffened. *Adorable?* It was her engagement ring, not a trinket. Tor had spent a lot of time finding just the right one, and it was absolutely everything Samantha wanted in a ring she was going to wear for the rest of her life.

"Beth and I have been discussing wedding themes," Erika continued, seemingly unaware that she had offended Samantha. "We agreed that given the season and your coloring, white and silver would be just right. Let me show you a few examples." She set her tea down and flipped open a large album, showing Samantha picture after picture of other weddings she had organized.

Samantha had to agree that the floral arrangements, the decorations, and the brides' dresses were fabulous. The more she looked at the tasteful photographs of radiant brides, stylish table settings, stunning multitiered cakes, engraved invitations, and fancy favors, the more she thought it might be fun to have a completely unforgettable, classy wedding.

"We'll have to rush on some of these things," Erika said, flipping open her pocket calendar. "I can meet you next Monday in Lexington so we can look at gowns, and I'll contact some florists to see what they can do for us, and then we'll need to decide on invitations and get them ordered. I'll leave you a couple of catalogs so you can look at cake designs and think about the gifts you'll want to give your maid of honor and bridesmaids. I have a list of photographers we can meet with, and of course you'll want to be with me to discuss the menu with the caterer." She smiled brightly. "This is a busy and exciting time for you, planning the most important day of your life!"

"Whew," Samantha said, her head reeling. "I never thought it could be this complicated."

Erika laughed softly and patted Samantha's knee. "Don't worry about a thing, dear. I'm very good at pulling it all together. I assure you, your wedding will go off without a hitch. It may seem like a lot, but I'll do the hard work. All you really need to worry about is how stunning you're going to look as you come down the aisle."

"Thank you," Samantha said, feeling a little like she'd just been run over by a horse. Erika picked up her things and Beth walked her out to the car while Samantha flipped through one of the catalogs, looking at cakes that made her think of white-frosted skyscrapers festooned with flowers and ribbons.

"It's a lot to go through, isn't it?" Beth said when she returned to the living room.

Samantha nodded and sighed. "That's understating it," she said. "I never realized how involved getting married could be."

"Don't worry," Beth said, sitting down beside her. "It's all going to be just perfect." She flipped open one of the magazines and pointed at a wedding cake. "Isn't that beautiful?"

For several minutes she looked through the magazines with Samantha, who wondered more and more how people managed to get married when it all seemed so complicated. When the phone rang, Beth jumped up to answer it, then returned to the room, looking distraught.

"Your dad said you need to get over to the barn quickly," she said. "He just called the vet for Shining. He thinks she's going into labor."

"No!" Samantha gasped in horror as she leaped from the sofa, catalogs skidding to the floor, Erika and the elegant wedding plans forgotten. "It's too soon!"

There couldn't be anything wrong with Shining. The mare was healthy and strong, and all of her pregnancies had gone so well. Beth must have misunderstood the message. Shining still had several months to go before she was ready to foal.

Samantha dashed outside, letting the cottage door slam shut behind her as she raced as fast as she could toward the broodmare barn, her heart thundering with fear for her beloved mare.

5

WHEN SAMANTHA REACHED THE BARN, SHE COULD SEE Mike and Len, Whitebrook's stable manager, standing at Shining's stall. Her father was coming out of the office, a tense frown creasing his brow.

"I don't know what's going on with her," he told Samantha as he fell in step beside her. "Vic found her circling in her stall and nipping at her sides. Dr. Smith is just down the road at the Bloomfields', so she'll be here soon."

As they hurried past Wonder, Fleet Goddess, Precocious, and Leap of Faith, Samantha barely noticed the other mares. Her only thought was of Shining and the unborn foal the mare was carrying.

"Oh, my poor Shining," she murmured when she

reached the stall. Shining was standing in the far corner of the stall, her head down and her ears flat, her sides heaving with every breath she took. As Samantha started to open the stall door, Shining pawed at the bedding underfoot, switching her tail back and forth irritably.

Before Samantha could slip inside, footsteps sounded from the far end of the barn, and she looked toward the barn door to see Dr. Smith striding down the aisle. The veterinarian hurried to the stall and stopped beside Mike.

"What's going on with her?" she asked, setting her bag down as she eyed the mare. Ian and Len quickly filled the vet in on Shining's symptoms. Dr. Smith nodded slowly.

"Let's have a look at your mare," she said to Samantha, waiting until the other woman had entered the stall before following her inside.

Samantha held Shining's head, petting the mare and murmuring softly to her while the vet examined her. After a few minutes Dr. Smith looked at Samantha, a deep frown marring her forehead. "It certainly appears that she's going into labor," she said.

"Can you stop it?" Samantha asked anxiously. "She's barely five months along."

Dr. Smith raised her shoulders. "I'm not sure,

Samantha," she said. "Sometimes nature has to take its course. But I'd like to take Shining to the clinic. I want her at the facility in case we need to perform emergency surgery."

Samantha continued to stroke Shining's neck. "It'll be okay, girl," she said quietly. "You're going to be fine." She only wished she believed what she was telling the mare.

"I'll have Vic get the trailer ready," Mike said, hurrying away.

Dr. Smith patted Shining's shoulder. "We'll do everything we can to save the foal and the mare, Samantha."

Her words struck a chord of fear in Samantha. "Even if she loses the foal, she'll be okay, right?" She couldn't imagine her life without Shining.

The vet looked her straight in the eye. "I don't want to give you false hope," she said. "But we'll do what we can, you know that."

Samantha exhaled and nodded. The vet picked up her bags, leaving Samantha in the stall with Shining, who stood with her head drooping and her eyes dull, her harsh breaths ringing loudly in Samantha's ears.

"I'm right here, Shining," Samantha murmured, unable to stop the tears that began to slip down her cheeks. She petted the mare's glossy chestnut coat gently. "You have to be all right, girl."

Len brought Shining's blanket and shipping boots, and Samantha helped him prepare her for the trip to the clinic. When she was ready to go, Ian held the stall door open, and Samantha slowly led the mare into the aisle.

"Shining's a fighter, Sammy," Ian said, covering her hand with his. "She's been through some tough times, but she's a strong horse."

"We'll hope for the best, right, Sammy?" Len said encouragingly.

Samantha bit at her lower lip and nodded. "Did you hear that, Shining?" she asked, stroking the mare's shoulder. "You have lots of people who care about you, and you're going to pull through this." Shining groaned quietly, pressing her head wearily against Samantha's side, then swung her head around to nip at her flank again.

"You poor girl," Samantha whispered. "Let's get you to the clinic so Dr. Smith can take care of you."

After Mike and Vic had left with Shining, Samantha went back to the house to call Tor.

"I'm so sorry, Sammy," he said when she told him about Shining. "Is there anything I can do?"

"Not right now," Samantha said, leaning against

the kitchen wall and closing her eyes. "I'm going over to the clinic. I can't even think about anything else until I know Shining is okay."

"I understand that," Tor said. "Call me if you need me."

"Thanks, Tor," Samantha said. After she hung up the phone she grabbed her purse and left the house, forcing herself to stay calm for the drive.

When she arrived at Dr. Smith's clinic, Max, Cindy's boyfriend, was in the office. As the veterinarian's son, he spent his free time helping his mother. Max planned to attend college to become a vet himself, and Samantha wondered if he had decided to go to New York for college so he and Cindy could be together, or if he would stay at home and attend the University of Kentucky. But she didn't want to be nosy, and right now all she could think of was Shining, anyway.

"She's in here, Samantha," Max said, leading her to the stalls in the back of the clinic. Samantha bit her lip when she saw Shining. Dr. Smith had already medicated the mare, who looked lethargic, her head drooping almost to the floor. Dr. Smith had set up a sling to keep her on her feet.

"Here's something to sit on," Max said, carrying a folding chair over for Samantha. "These are good accommodations for horses, but they aren't the most comfortable for humans."

"I don't care," Samantha replied. "I just need to be with her."

The vet came in several times to check on Shining, but each time she left the stall she shook her head, discouraged. "It doesn't look good, Sammy," she said, standing by the stall door, her stethoscope hanging out of the pocket of her white lab coat. "But all we can do is wait and keep a close eye on her."

"I'm not leaving her side," Samantha said.

"I'll have Max bring in a cot," Dr. Smith told her. "You're free to spend the night here. I'll be in my office."

Through the long night, Samantha tried to lie down and close her eyes, but she was too wound up and distraught to fall asleep. Every time Shining shifted her weight, Samantha was on her feet, checking on the mare. But nothing changed, and Samantha lay down on the cot, staring at the darkness pressing against the window. *Maybe this will pass,* she thought. *Shining may not lose the foal after all.*

Finally, as the sun was starting to shine through the windows that lined one wall, Dr. Smith returned to the room. "You need to go home and get some sleep," she said, eyeing Samantha with a motherly expression. "It isn't going to do Shining any good for you to collapse from exhaustion. If anything changes, I'll call you immediately."

Samantha started to protest, but Dr. Smith folded her arms and frowned. "Once we're through the worst of this, she's going to need all the care and attention you can give her," she said. "Go home and get some rest." She offered Samantha a sympathetic smile. "That's an order."

Reluctantly Samantha gave Shining a pat, but the mare didn't even respond to her. Samantha left the clinic feeling despondent over Shining's well-being. By the time she reached Whitebrook, she was drained. There was no one in the cottage, so she stumbled upstairs and dropped onto her bed without bothering to change into her pajamas.

She slept heavily, a deep, dreamless sleep, and when she opened her eyes, she was shocked to see that it was well past noon. Samantha's mind struggled to clear itself, and immediately she thought of Shining.

She snapped back to reality and leaped from the bed, her hair tangled and her clothes rumpled, to hurry downstairs to call the clinic.

Before she could pick up the receiver, the phone rang, and Samantha snatched it from the hook. "Hello?" she said, bracing herself.

"Hey, Sammy," Tor said. "I just wanted to find out how things were going."

"I don't know yet," Samantha said, sighing wearily. "I'm going to call the clinic right now."

"Keep me posted, okay?" Tor asked. "I'll come over as soon as I'm done with lessons this afternoon."

"Thanks, Tor," Samantha said, hanging up the phone.

She dialed the clinic's number, and when Max answered the phone she asked to speak to his mother.

"Just a sec," Max said, and Samantha waited anxiously for Dr. Smith to get on the line. It seemed like an eternity before the vet picked up the phone.

"I just left Shining," the vet told her when she finally answered the call. "I'm sorry, Samantha, but Shining lost the foal she was carrying."

"What about Shining?" Samantha asked, a sinking feeling washing over her. "Is she all right?"

"As far as I can tell, she's doing okay," the vet said. "We'll keep her here for a couple of days and make certain there aren't any problems, but I'm confident she's going to pull through." She paused.

"Is there something else?" Samantha asked, her throat tightening.

"She suffered some damage," Dr. Smith said. "I don't think she'll ever be able to carry another foal."

"I don't care," Samantha said immediately. "I just want her to be all right. Even if she could have another one, I don't think I'd want to ever breed her again." After Samantha hung up the phone, she called Tor to tell him what was going on. When no one answered the phone at Whisperwood, she left a message, then headed to the barn to tell her father and Ashleigh what had happened. But when she saw Brad Townsend's sports car parked near the broodmare barn, Samantha cringed. Brad was the last person she wanted to see right now.

She slipped into the stallion barn instead, hoping to catch her father there. She saw Cindy at Wonder's Champion's stall, feeding the fiery chestnut a carrot. Cindy had the same close bond with Champion that Samantha had with Pride, Champion's younger half brother. But Champion tended to be unruly, while Pride was a much more personable stallion.

When Cindy saw her, she left Champion and met Samantha in the middle of the barn. "I'm really sorry about Shining," she said.

As Samantha started to ask how she knew about the mare, Ashleigh stepped out of the office, Brad and Lavinia right behind her. Samantha groaned. The Townsends owned Shining's sire, Townsend Pride, and Brad always seemed to make any horse with Townsend bloodlines his business. But Brad's interest in the horses was purely financial, and Samantha knew that if Shining was his, he would get rid of her in a heartbeat. A broodmare who couldn't produce had no value to Brad.

At least I have full ownership of Shining, Samantha told herself, trying to find something positive in the situation despite the sad news the vet had given her.

From the stall closest to where Samantha and Cindy were standing, Wonder's Pride nickered softly to her, and Samantha reached out to pet his muscular neck. Much of the bad feelings Samantha had toward Brad Townsend stemmed from the years Pride was being raced, when the Townsends had pushed Ashleigh to ride the colt much harder than was good for him. A talented Thoroughbred, Pride had won both the Kentucky Derby and the Preakness, and even though he was exhausted from the tough campaign, he'd placed a respectable second in the Belmont Stakes.

"Dr. Smith called to let me know what happened," Ashleigh said, giving Samantha a warning look.

Samantha sighed. Obviously the news had come while the Townsends were in the office, so Brad knew exactly what was going on.

"What a pity about Shining," Brad said. "She dropped some decent foals."

Samantha exhaled and nodded. She didn't have the energy to argue with Brad. Shining's foals were far better than "decent," but she wasn't going to let Brad get to her. "At least I still have Lucky Chance," she said. "And Shining will always have a good home with me."

Lavinia raised her chin slightly and looked down her nose at Samantha, the expression on her face one of disgust. Samantha braced herself for one of Lavinia's cutting remarks, then winced. She had left the house without so much as running a brush through her hair, let alone changing out of the clothes she had slept in. Lavinia could probably smell her. Samantha sensed Cindy stiffen beside her. Samantha caught Ashleigh's eye, and her friend gave her a tiny wink and a smile. Bolstered by Cindy and Ashleigh's presence, Samantha relaxed. What did she care about Lavinia's opinion, anyway?

"Nice to see you, Lavinia," she said, giving the other woman a cool smile. She stepped forward, blocking Cindy's view of Brad's young wife. She was sure that given the slightest excuse, her sister would tear into Lavinia, who had done malicious things when Cindy was a foster child at the McLeans', but the last thing Samantha needed was to be in the middle of a fight between Cindy and Lavinia.

Lavinia pinched her lips in a false smile, then turned to Ashleigh. "You do realize how important it is for you to make an appearance at the club for this event, don't you? Since you have an interest in Wonder and her foals, people will expect to see you."

Ashleigh nodded. "I told you I'd be there, Lavinia," she said, sounding a little irritable. "Now I do have work to do here, so if you'll excuse me . . ."

"Of course," Lavinia said haughtily. "We have things to do too, don't we, darling?" She turned to Brad, offering him a bright smile.

For a moment her expression was transformed. Samantha stared openly, seeing Lavinia differently as she gazed at her husband, a warmth in her eyes that Samantha would never have expected coming from Lavinia.

She does love him, Samantha thought, startled at the idea of Lavinia caring about anyone but herself.

Brad smiled at his wife and nodded, then turned to Ashleigh. "We'll see you on December seventh at the club," he said. "Don't forget, it's a black-tie affair." He took Lavinia's hand, and they strode out of the barn.

Samantha froze. December seventh was the date Beth had booked the club for the wedding.

"What are the Townsends doing at the country club?" Samantha asked.

"They came by to tell me about a holiday party they're having for several Thoroughbred owners. Brad wants to promote the Townsends' breeding stock, and when it involves Wonder and her foals, I am a part of the whole thing. There's no way to get out of going."

"That's your wedding day, Sammy," Cindy protested, propping her fisted hands on her hips. "They can't take that away from you. You can't let them!"

"I'll call the club and double-check on the dates," Samantha said calmly. "There may have been a mix-up." She was pretty sure there hadn't been.

"I'm going to go check on the yearlings," Cindy said, scowling toward the barn door, where the sound of Brad's sports car roaring to life echoed down the aisle. "I need a dose of colts and fillies to get Brad and Lavinia off my mind." She stalked out of the barn, and Ashleigh shook her head, watching her go.

"She really doesn't like the Townsends, does she?" she said in a mild voice. "We need to encourage

75

her to express her feelings a little more openly."

Samantha stared at her for a minute, thinking Ashleigh was serious. But when Ashleigh smiled wryly, Samantha couldn't help but chuckle. "She says what the rest of us think," she said. "I just prefer having nothing to do with them at all."

Footsteps in the aisle had Samantha cringing again, thinking Brad and Lavinia had returned. But when she looked toward the door, Tor was hurrying toward her, a worried look on his face.

"I got your message," he said when he reached her. He opened his arms wide and pulled her into a strong embrace. "I'm so sorry, Sammy. What a rotten thing to happen."

Samantha nodded against his chest. "But Shining will get through it," she said. "It would have been so much worse if I'd lost her, too."

"I'm going over to the training barn," Ashleigh said. "I need to tell Mike about the Townsends' little get-together, and I'll let your dad know about Shining, Sammy."

After she left the barn, Samantha told Tor about the party Brad and Lavinia had scheduled. They went into the barn office, and Samantha dialed the number of the country club. After a brief conversation, she hung up the phone and turned to Tor.

"We're not having the wedding at the club," she said, not sure if she was disappointed or relieved. "Apparently someone double-booked the banquet hall, and Brad and Lavinia get priority treatment. It just figures." She tipped her head back and exhaled. "Now we need to set a new date. I'm glad we didn't order invitations or anything yet."

Tor smiled. "You really didn't want to get married at the club anyway," he said easily. "And it isn't like we have to have the wedding in December. We can put off setting a new date for a little while. At least until you get Shining home and things calm down."

"I'm glad you're so understanding," Samantha said.

"Maybe we could just elope," Tor suggested, the twinkle in his eyes telling Samantha he was teasing.

But at the moment it didn't sound like such a bad idea to Samantha. "I do much better organizing horse shows for the Pony Commandos than trying to put a wedding together," she said.

Tor chuckled. "We could just take off," he said, then grinned. "On horseback."

"Don't tempt me," Samantha said dryly. "I might take you up on it."

"Everyone we know would have a posse after us," Tor said, shaking his head. "We can't sneak off and get married without inviting all our family and friends."

"We can keep it really simple, though," Samantha said. "Let's use the little chapel in Lexington and have a quiet ceremony. We really don't need a party at the country club."

"I'll set it up with a minister I know in town," Tor said immediately. "If you're sure you want a small wedding, then I'm all for it."

"Right now that's all I can deal with," Samantha said. Now that she had decided against a grand celebration, she felt a little let down. She hadn't thought it would mean that much to her, but she hoped she wouldn't regret the choice. But the important thing was that she and Tor would be married. Nothing else really mattered, right?

6

"A SMALL WEDDING?" BETH REPEATED WHEN SAMANTHA told her about Brad and Lavinia's party at the country club. Beth stood in the middle of the kitchen, her hands dusted with flour from the loaf of whole-wheat bread she was kneading. She frowned and swiped at her forehead, leaving a streak of flour on her brow. "I hate to see the Townsends spoil this for you. Are you sure you're okay with it?"

Samantha nodded. "It'll be just fine," she said firmly. "It won't be as expensive, and Tor and I will be perfectly happy." She took a clean dish towel and wiped the flour off Beth's face, then leaned back against the counter, cocked her head to the side, and folded her arms. "Face it, Beth," she said, smiling.

"We're not really country-club-type folks anyway."

Beth pinched her lips together, trying not to laugh. "You've made your point," she said, patting Samantha's hand, leaving a floury handprint behind. "It's just that it's such a special day, and I want it to be just right."

Ignoring the flour-dusted apron Beth was wearing, Samantha gave her stepmother a hug. "I know you do," she said. "But Tor and I agreed this is what we want. And we decided to wait until February. That way the Chase for Charity will be over, and most of the mares will have foaled. It'll work out great."

Beth laughed and shook her head. "Of course you'd want to schedule it around the horses," she said. "I don't know why I imagined you would think any other way."

Samantha wiped the front of her shirt and jeans with the towel and handed it to Beth. "I'm glad you understand," she said. "Now I'm heading over to the clinic to check on Shining. Tor's going to meet me there."

When she got to the clinic, Tor's truck was already parked in the lot. Samantha walked inside to see Mandy sitting on the edge of a chair in the waiting room, a card and a small bouquet of colorful flowers in her hands.

"I hope it's okay that I made Tor bring me here," Mandy said quickly. "I had to see Shining."

Samantha smiled at the girl. "Of course," she said. "I know she'll be glad to see you."

"Tor's talking to the vet," Mandy told her, holding out the card and flowers. "I wanted to bring her a treat, but I didn't know what she could eat right now, so I brought these instead."

Samantha opened the handmade card. Mandy had drawn a picture of a chestnut horse on the front, standing in a white-fenced meadow of grass and flowers, with the sun shining brightly overhead. On the inside she had written simply *I love you, Shining* and signed it.

Samantha felt tears well up in her eyes, and she blinked rapidly, trying to get her emotions under control. "This is really sweet, Mandy," she said. "And the picture looks exactly like Shining."

Mandy blushed a little. "I wanted to draw her looking happy," she said. "She will be again, I'm sure of it."

"And you did a great job," Samantha reassured her. "Now let's go see her."

When they followed Shawna, Dr. Smith's regular assistant, to the back of the clinic, Samantha was distressed at how Shining looked. The mare's eyes were

still dull and lifeless. She hoped seeing Shining looking so awful wouldn't upset Mandy, who adored the
mare.

But Mandy stepped past Samantha and went into
the stall quietly, holding her hand out so that Shining
could sniff her palm. The mare sighed. "You'll be
home soon, and we'll get you nice and healthy
again."

Samantha smiled to herself. Mandy's love for
Shining was unconditional. With her help, they
would nurse Shining back to health in no time.

Dr. Smith and Tor came into the stable and stood
by Samantha, watching Mandy pet Shining.

"She looks a little better just having the company,"
the vet observed while Mandy continued to stroke
the mare's neck and murmur softly to her.

As Samantha watched Mandy comfort the horse,
an idea began to bloom in her mind. "When can we
bring her home?" she asked the vet.

"Monday at the earliest," Dr. Smith said, her eyes
still on the girl and the horse. "I don't want to take
any chances. As soon as I'm sure she's stable, you can
take her back to Whitebrook."

Tor looked from Mandy and Shining to Samantha,
and Samantha could sense that he was thinking along
the same lines as she was.

After they left the clinic, Samantha followed Tor and Mandy back to Whisperwood, her thoughts on Shining and how much Mandy cared about her. When they got to the Nelsons' farm, Mandy immediately went to the feed room for a handful of carrots and went out to give the Pony Commando horses each a treat.

Samantha turned to Tor as Mandy left the barn. "Do you think—" she started to say as Tor opened his mouth.

"Maybe you should—" he said.

They both stopped talking. "You first," Tor said.

"Do you think I could bring Shining here instead of Whitebrook?" she asked.

Tor grinned. "I was just going to suggest the same thing," he said, looking out the barn door to where Mandy was feeding Zorro a chunk of carrot. As they watched, Mrs. Jarvis pulled up by the barn. Mandy turned and waved to her mother as she got out of her car. When Mrs. Jarvis walked over to the fence, Mandy handed her a carrot, and Mrs. Jarvis leaned over the fence to scratch Milk Dud behind the ears. She fed the little brown pony a piece of carrot as she laughed at something Mandy said.

"Mandy loves Shining as much as I do," Samantha said.

"She really seemed to perk up when Mandy was with her today," Tor agreed. "I think it would be good for both of them to spend some time together, and since Mandy is here to ride so much anyway, it would work out great."

"I can come over every day to take care of her medications," Samantha said. "I'm sure Dr. Smith will have a list of things that will need to be done."

Tor nodded. "I like that idea," he said. "Shining will get lots of love from Mandy and good care from you."

Samantha visited Shining at the clinic daily, and on Monday she hitched the horse trailer to her father's pickup and drove to the clinic.

"You look a hundred percent better already," she told Shining when she went into the stable, where Dr. Smith was waiting.

"Now that she won't be a broodmare, I guess I need to focus on her training as a saddle horse," Samantha told the vet. "I've ridden her some, but she's still a racehorse at heart. It'll be good for her to learn some new skills."

Dr. Smith nodded in agreement. "For all practical purposes she's a green-broke horse," she said. "She knows how to take a rider, and she'll run, but as you well know, there's a whole lot more she needs to learn." Dr. Smith gazed at Shining, who had her head over the stall door, trying to lip at Samantha's sleeve. "But she has a good disposition," Dr. Smith continued. "I'm sure she'd make an excellent all-around riding horse."

Samantha brought her out of the stall, and Dr. Smith walked with them out to the trailer. "I'll come to check on her in a couple of days," she said, holding the trailer door while Samantha led the mare inside and clipped the tie to Shining's halter.

"Thanks for all you help," Samantha said, climbing into the truck. Dr. Smith waved good-bye and turned to go back into the clinic, and Samantha headed down the road.

When Samantha reached Whisperwood, Mandy was outside the barn, waiting for them. "I'll put her in her stall," Mandy offered eagerly when Samantha led Shining from the trailer. "I have it all fixed up for her, with lots of thick bedding and fresh water." She patted Shining's neck. "I'm so glad you're here," she told the mare, kissing her soft nose.

"Here you go," Samantha said, handing Mandy Shining's lead. She stood by the trailer and watched the girl lead the mare away. Samantha realized that when Mandy was walking the horse, her limp was barely noticeable.

As Mandy and Shining disappeared through the barn door, Tor came out to where Samantha was leaning against the fender of the truck. "You should see how Mandy fixed up the stall. Shining is going to think she's royalty," he said.

"She is," Samantha said firmly. "And Mandy will make sure she knows it."

Tor draped his arm across Samantha's shoulders and smiled down at her, then reached over to catch her left hand with his right one. He ran his finger over the engagement ring, then looked at Samantha. "Now that Shining is going to be okay, we can get back to our wedding plans, right?"

"Nothing more involved than a few friends and a quiet ceremony," Samantha reminded him. "And we have months to make sure everything goes right. Besides that," she added with a grin, "we don't have to worry about the Townsends wanting to use the little chapel for one of their get-togethers, so I think our date is safe."

Tor nodded thoughtfully. "If you still want to have a fancier wedding . . ." He gazed at her steadily.

Samantha promptly shook her head. She had gotten caught up in the idea of a showy ceremony for a while, but she was past that now. "Quiet and small will be perfect," she said, smiling up at Tor. "Meanwhile, how is Sierra doing? Do you want to take him and Top Hat out for a hack? I think they could both use the exercise."

"Good idea," Tor said enthusiastically. "But first you need to see what Mandy did with Shining's stall." He took Samantha's hand and led her through the barn, to the row of stalls on the far side.

When they reached Mandy and Shining, Samantha was impressed at how much work Mandy had done to set up a comfortable place for the mare. Mandy was in the stall with Shining, petting her while she sniffed at the walls, then took a drink from the water bucket.

"She's going to do fine here," Mandy announced. "I'll spend time with her every day."

After Mrs. Jarvis came to pick Mandy up, Tor and Samantha saddled Sierra and Top Hat and headed out on one of the trails behind Whisperwood.

Samantha sat easily to Sierra's extended trot, enjoying the brisk fall weather. The chestnut horse snorted, tossing his head, and Samantha patted his neck. "You sure do feel frisky," she said.

Beside her on Top Hat, Tor was relaxed, a contented look on his face. "We need to do this more often," he said, a smile curling at his lips. "We don't get to ride together nearly enough."

"I agree," Samantha said. "It's too bad we can't take the horses with us on our honeymoon."

"We can probably rent horses and ride on the beach," Tor suggested. "I'll look into it."

As they rode down the trail, Samantha tilted her head toward another path that branched off the main trail. The spur, wide and clear, seemed to call to her.

"Let's pick up the pace," she said, nodding toward the grassy lane.

"You're on," Tor said, perking up in the saddle. "But remember, Top Hat isn't a racehorse, he's a show jumper. Try not to leave us too far behind."

"We'll pace ourselves," Samantha promised. She kept a firm grip on the reins, knowing that Sierra would break into a hard gallop if he was given a chance. She scanned the trail ahead for any obstacles so that she could keep Sierra from performing any unplanned steeplechase moves.

They cantered down the path, which wound through the trees, ending in a large, open meadow. As Samantha circled Sierra around the clearing, she felt him jerk his head, and she spotted the downed tree a split second after he did. "No, you don't!" she cried, hauling at the rein before Sierra could go off at a gallop. The horse snorted and scooted his hindquarters to the side, trying to aim them in the direction of the jump.

Tor rode Top Hat over to the tree and checked out the far side. Then he looked back at Samantha. "It looks good on this side if you want to try it," he offered.

Sierra yanked at the bit, straining to get loose and run. "Sierra's dying to go over it," she said. "I guess we have to or he'll never forgive me." Samantha turned Sierra away from the jump and moved him into a canter, circling the large meadow again, and as they came around to face the jump, Sierra sped up, stretching into a racing gallop. Samantha leaned forward on his shoulders, watching the distance as they closed in on the tree. As they reached the takeoff point, she felt Sierra's powerful muscles bunch and suddenly they were airborne.

The feeling of weightlessness seemed to last forever before the horse landed cleanly on the other side, and Samantha circled the meadow again as she slowed him, then rode up to Tor, a grin stretching across her face.

Tor applauded, nodding his approval. "Excellent jump," he said. "You should have seen yourself."

"It felt perfect," Samantha agreed. "I can hardly

wait to take him on the course they're setting up at Bright Meadows."

"I'm looking forward to watching you race him," Tor said. "That's going to be a fun day."

"And the Brightons are doing such a great job in promoting it," Samantha said. "They have enough entries to schedule seven races, and found sponsors to donate trophies and prizes for the awards."

"I think it's time we headed back," Tor said, glancing at his watch. "This has been the best afternoon I've had in a long time."

"Me too," Samantha said, turning Sierra toward the path that led back to Whisperwood. As they rode back in companionable silence Samantha felt contented and relaxed. At the farm they put the horses up, and Samantha went to visit Shining before she left for home, giving the mare her doses of medication. Tor began taking care of his afternoon responsibilities at the barn.

"I had a really nice time," Samantha said, sticking her head inside the office door, where Tor was making some notes about the following day's lessons.

"I'll see you tomorrow afternoon, right?" Tor told her, giving her a kiss good-bye.

"Every day," Samantha confirmed.

When she got home, the answering machine was

blinking, and Samantha pressed the play button, wincing when she heard Erika Alfonso's irritated tone.

"Samantha," Erika's message began, "we were scheduled to meet at the bridal shop hours ago. I waited as long as I could. I don't know how you expect me to organize your wedding if you don't cooperate."

Samantha groaned and scrubbed her face with her hands. After Brad and Lavinia had forced her to change her wedding plans, she'd forgotten about Erika. Worrying about Shining had driven thoughts of the wedding planner completely from her mind. But Samantha was pretty sure Erika wouldn't understand about the horses. And now that the wedding date had been postponed and the grand plans canceled, she didn't really need to have Erika's help.

She dialed the wedding planner's number and left a message, apologizing for her thoughtlessness. Beth walked into the kitchen as she hung up the phone, and Samantha explained about the missed appointment.

"I'll speak to her," Beth said reassuringly. "But it is true, now that we have a little more time and aren't making it quite as involved, we can do this ourselves. It would be fun if I could take you shopping for your dress." She hesitated. "Unless you'd rather do it yourself, or with Yvonne and Ashleigh."

"Of course I'd like to do it with you!" Samantha exclaimed. "I'd much rather spend the time with you picking out the right dress than anyone else." She was rewarded with a pleased smile from Beth.

The next couple of weeks flew by. Samantha was busy running between Whisperwood, where Shining was thriving under Mandy's care, her work at Whitebrook, and taking care of some of the details for the upcoming Bright Meadows steeplechase event.

On the morning of the Bright Meadows steeplechase Samantha met Tor at Whisperwood. He already had Sierra's tack in the trailer and was getting the big horse ready for the trip to the sport horse farm near Versailles.

"I can't believe it's already October," Samantha said, patting Sierra's nose. She looked around, noticing the changing trees, and started to laugh. "I haven't taken the time to stop and smell the roses, and they're already done blooming!"

Tor swept her into his arms. "When we go on our honeymoon," he told her, "we'll plan a month-long vacation. You're going to need it."

"That sounds wonderful," Samantha said.

When they reached Bright Meadows, there were already several trucks and trailers parked in the large field the Brightons had designated for the parking lot. Tor pulled up beside a small, older trailer.

The Bright Meadows grounds were abuzz with trainers, owners, and jockeys, and the air rang with the shrill whinnies of the horses being unloaded. Samantha felt a rush of excitement, caught up in the high energy of race day.

"Look at all the people!" she exclaimed, gazing around at the crowded parking lot. "The Brightons did an amazing job setting up this fund-raiser for the Pony Commandos."

"They sure did," Tor agreed. "This is really going to help us out a lot."

"The competition looks pretty stiff," Samantha commented, watching a woman lead a massive gray horse toward the racecourse. "I hope Sierra and I do okay."

"You're going to be awesome out there," Tor told her, leaning across the seat to give her a kiss on the cheek. "I'll go check in with the officials if you want to take care of Sierra."

When they climbed from the truck, Tor took off for the tented area, where volunteers were checking the horses and riders in, and Samantha went to the back of the trailer to unload Sierra.

As she reached for the latch she looked to her side and froze. Tied to the battered trailer beside them was the biggest Thoroughbred she had ever seen. The mare's dark chestnut coat gleamed red in the morning sun, and her large, bright eyes seemed to take in everything going on around her. But as Samantha looked over the mare's conformation, she frowned. Her height was right for a jumper, and she seemed well built for flat-track racing. *It will be interesting to watch her on the racecourse,* Samantha thought, admiring the big horse.

"She's a Man o' War descendant," a voice from behind her said.

Samantha turned to see a middle-aged man lugging a bucket of water to the trailer. "She's huge," Samantha said, glancing back at the mare. "Do you call her Big Red, the same way they did Man o' War?"

He shook his head. "Her name is Miss Battleship," he said. "Her great-grandsire was Battleship, the Man o' War colt who won the Grand National steeplechase."

"Which race is she scheduled for?" Samantha asked, instantly interested in the big mare.

"Fifth race," the man said. "If my jockey shows

up." He scowled at his watch. "This will be the third race she's run, and so far she isn't panning out. I bought her expecting to have a good chaser, but she's been a real disappointment for me."

"Good luck," Samantha replied, then unlatched Tor's trailer to get Sierra out. The horse, a veteran of several steeplechases, didn't seem too excited about the people and animals milling around. Since Sierra was competing in the first race of the day, she needed to get him ready to ride.

Tor returned with a handful of papers, and he and Samantha went through the day's program. "It's going to be a great day," he said with a grin. "The jumps look pretty straightforward, and I know Sierra's going to sail right through."

"I want to watch that mare race," Samantha said, pointing to the big red horse.

Tor eyed Miss Battleship and nodded. "She looks pretty good," he said. "I'm glad you're not riding against her. I'll be she can fly."

Samantha saw several people she knew and spent a little time before her race visiting, thanking the fans for supporting the fund-raising event before she climbed into the trailer's tack room to change into her Whitebrook silks.

When it came time to mount up, Samantha took a

deep breath, looking over the dozen horses in the field. "Wish me luck," she told Tor.

Tor planted a kiss on her forehead before she pulled her helmet into place. "You'll be perfect out there," he said. "Both of you will."

Samantha rode Sierra to the starting line and circled the eager horse, keeping him from taking off before the starting flag dropped. As she brought his nose forward she caught the flash of bright silk as the starter began the race. Samantha leaned over Sierra's shoulders as they plunged into a hard run, shoulder to shoulder with the jumpers on either side of them.

7

SAMANTHA ROSE IN THE STIRRUPS, IGNORING THE HORSES crowding them on both sides. Even though there were no purses for that day's races, she still felt the excitement of competition, and she wanted Sierra to win. "Come on, boy," she urged him, looking ahead to the first fence. "Let's show the rest of these horses what a top-notch horse can do."

Samantha had walked the course while she was working with the Brightons to organize the event, but none of the horses had been on it. That was part of the excitement and challenge of riding a steeplechase.

Sierra flicked his ears back, listening to her, and he dug into the turf, fighting the rest of the field to move into a better position. As they neared the jump,

Samantha settled into jumping position, feeling Sierra's powerful muscles bunch as he prepared to soar into the air. They sailed over the four-foot brush wall as though it weren't even there, and Sierra surged forward.

Don't rush at the start. Pace yourself—save something for the second half of the race, Samantha told herself, running Tor's instructions through her head. She tried to figure how much Sierra would need to hold back in order to finish the grueling course.

The cheering crowd and the voice of the announcer calling the race layered over the sounds of hooves pounding the turf, the snorted breaths of the other horses, and the voices of the jockeys as they encouraged their horses. As they approached the second jump, a wide, water-filled ditch, the gray to Sierra's right seemed to be veering toward them. Samantha shot a quick look to her side, concerned about how near the other horse was. With such a tightly packed field, if one horse stumbled or went down it could easily interfere with other racers. That, she reminded herself, was part of steeplechasing. She quickly looked ahead again, forcing herself not to think about the risks.

As Sierra stretched his legs and cleared the water, Samantha rose in the stirrups again, asking the horse for more speed on the flat. The mile-long course, laid out in a sprawling valley on the Brightons' sport horse farm, stretched ahead of them. Three riders had already pulled ahead of the rest of the field, and Samantha felt Sierra tug at the reins, trying to speed up so he could catch the front-runners.

"Easy," she murmured, holding him back. "We have a two-mile run and twenty fences to jump. We have plenty of time to win this one, so let's not rush things."

Sierra strained against the hold she had on him, trying to pick up the pace, and Samantha worried that he would put so much energy into fighting her that he wouldn't have what he needed to finish. "Have a little patience," she admonished him, feeling the taut reins pulling against her grip.

They hurdled the next two jumps easily, still running with the pack, but as they started into the curve of the track, a riderless horse charged by them, its head high, the reins flapping against its neck. Sierra rolled his eye at the passing horse and fought Samantha to let him catch up. *I hope the rider is okay*, Samantha thought as the horse thundered up the course, flying over some jumps and dodging around others.

The next jump, a five-foot-high, five-foot-wide wall of brush, loomed ahead of them and Samantha struggled to keep Sierra's attention on the obstacle instead of the loose animal. She breathed a sigh of relief when they soared over the fence and followed the track as it circled along the backstretch. "Two more easy jumps, then another big one," she said, letting Sierra pick up his pace. They closed in on the three lead horses as they galloped along the flat stretch, popping over the low jumps almost as though they weren't there.

The long flat before the next big fence gave Samantha a chance to glance behind her. She could see that several horses hadn't made it through the first series of fences. As far as she could tell, at least six horses had left the track. She looked forward again, patting Sierra's neck as he galloped strongly toward the high brush wall. Samantha knew there was a drop on the other side of the wall, but with Sierra's experience, she was confident that he wouldn't be thrown off by the change in terrain.

As the lead horses flew over the jump, they disappeared from view for a moment, then Samantha saw two of the riders gallop on, which meant there was a horse down on the other side of the fence. She angled Sierra to the left, going for the inside of the jump, hoping they could avoid a wreck with the horse and rider she knew were on the other side. Sierra lunged up, rising over the five-foot wall, but as they were clearing the obstacle, Samantha saw the horse just to their right, scrambling to its feet, and she caught her breath, afraid the animal would bump Sierra. Distracted, she bounced forward onto her horse's shoulders as they came down onto the lower side of the jump.

Sierra stumbled, and Samantha gripped his mane with both hands and tightened her legs on his sides, trying to stay in the saddle. As he struggled to keep his feet several horses ran by, putting Sierra back into seventh place. But just when she thought they were going to fall, the determined horse righted himself and took off running after the rest of the horses.

Samantha darted another look behind to see that three riders had fallen at the drop, but they were all on their feet. Two of the riders were frantically trying to remount, and the third was leading his horse off the course. She turned her attention back to the race.

"We're halfway there," she told Sierra, moving into jumping position again as they approached another fence.

They were closing in on the water jump for the second time, and Sierra was still running strongly. Samantha could feel the energy he had left, and she let him open up a bit, narrowing the lead of the horses in front of them. Sierra flew across the water jump and sped up again, then popped over the low fences as though he hadn't just run a tough mile on the course.

"You still have lots left, don't you?" Samantha asked him, feeling the horse lengthen his strides on the flat. She gave him a little more rein, elated as he closed the gap between them and the front-runners.

Soon they were coming back around to the difficult jump that had taken out so many horses. Samantha could see several of the lead horses flagging as the distance and the challenge of the jumps took its toll. Sierra blew past three horses bunched together, leaped over another low fence, and dug in to catch up with the remaining two horses.

As they neared the big fence Sierra's nose was at the shoulder of the lead horse, a big black. By the time they took off to clear the fence, the two horses were nose to nose. Samantha held her breath as they came over the wall, doing everything she could not to impede Sierra. When they landed cleanly, she let out a whoosh of pent-up air. Sierra landed ahead of the black, and Samantha rose in the stirrups and crouched over his shoulders, giving the horse enough rein to gallop freely.

As they crossed the finish line, she knew they had

won the race. The crowd on the sidelines applauded and cheered, and Samantha circled Sierra, who was acting as though he could run the course a third time rather than stop.

She saw Tor hurrying toward them, grinning broadly. Samantha brought Sierra to a stop, and Tor caught the horse's bridle, then slapped her on the knee. "Great job!" he exclaimed. "Awesome ride, Sammy, just awesome."

"That was pretty intense," she said breathlessly as she hopped off Sierra. Her legs wobbled a bit when she hit the ground, and she leaned against Tor. "Sierra's in great shape, but if I'm going to keep riding like this, I need to work out more."

Tor nodded. "People don't really appreciate how demanding it is," he agreed. "Why don't you go rest up a bit, and I'll walk Sierra out for you before the award presentation."

Samantha shook her head. "The trophy we won isn't for me," she said. "It needs to go to the Pony Commandos. I'm just glad I won it for the club."

Tor smiled at her. "Good call," he said approvingly.

After the awards ceremony, Mrs. Brighton announced that the gate money and entry fees had raised several thousand dollars to help the Pony

Commandos. Samantha and Tor walked away from the officials' stand and headed for the trailer.

"Excuse me, miss." Samantha turned to see Miss Battleship's owner beside her. "That was an impressive ride," he said. "You handled your horse very well."

"Thanks," Samantha said.

"I was wondering if you'd take my mare out for the fifth race," he continued. "My jockey never did show up."

Samantha hesitated. She would love to race again, but she didn't know the horse.

"You have plenty of time," Tor interjected. "The second race is just getting set up now. It'll be a couple of hours before the fifth race is run."

"Why don't you try her out, then decide," the owner urged.

"Okay," Samantha said. The idea of riding the Man o' War mare was too tempting to resist, and she followed the owner back to his trailer, where the big red mare was still tied.

Samantha helped tack the mare, then took her to a paddock away from the track and mounted up. The mare was quick and responsive, and after several minutes Samantha nodded. "I'll do it," she said. "I'll race her."

When the fifth race was lining up, she circled the mare, waiting for the starting flag to drop. When it did, she leaned over Miss Battleship's withers. The mare plunged over the starting line, joining the pack of steeplechasers as they started the course.

Right away they were boxed in, but Miss Battleship ran gamely, squeezing herself into a gap between two of the horses in front of them. When they reached the first jump the mare gathered herself and neatly cleared the jump, but she pulled up as they landed, slowing her pace instead of speeding up.

Samantha rose in the stirrups and pushed her into a hard gallop. The mare responded willingly, but as they rode the course, Samantha knew they would be doing well by not finishing last. The mare's jumping style was clean and powerful, and she was a strong runner, but she just didn't seem to put the jumping together with the flat racing.

As they crossed the finish line in sixth place, Samantha patted Miss Battleship's sweaty shoulder. "You did good," she consoled the mare. "You just need more training."

The owner was waiting for them, a glum look on his face. "I never should have bought her," he said, shaking his head as he held the mare so that Samantha could dismount.

"She's great," Samantha argued. "She just needs more experience."

He eyed the mare. "I have two other horses that do much better," he said. "I wanted to give her one last chance, but I promised myself that this would be it. I guess she'll be going to the auction." He smiled at Samantha. "Thanks for riding her," he said, then led the mare away.

Samantha watched them walk off as Tor came up beside her.

"Did you feel what I saw?" he asked.

Samantha glanced at him. "She can run, and she can jump, but not at the same time," she said.

Tor nodded. "That was it," he agreed. "She has perfect style when she's jumping, and she's fast as a bullet. There has to be a way to help her pull it all together."

"He's going to sell her," Samantha told him, then eyed him expectantly.

"I have money put away, but it's for our honeymoon," Tor replied.

"Me too," Samantha said.

"How badly do you want to go to the Caribbean?"

Samantha angled her head and pursed her lips. "She'd be a great mare to have," she said. "Man o' War bloodlines and a Grand National winner in the family tree? We can always take our trip for an anniversary instead."

"Let's go talk to him," Tor said, catching Samantha by the hand.

When they left Bright Meadows that afternoon, Samantha and Tor co-owned Miss Battleship, and Tor had made arrangements to pick up the mare.

The following Saturday, Mandy was already at Whisperwood when Samantha got to the farm.

"Shining's doing tons better," Mandy informed Samantha, leading her to the mare's stall. "See at how good she looks?" The mare's eyes were bright and clear, and Mandy had groomed her until her coat was glossy.

"You're the best nurse she could ever have," Samantha told Mandy. "I'm so glad you're taking care of her." As they watched, the mare rubbed her upper lip on the stall wall, then nudged her feed pan and eyed Samantha.

"She looks a little bored," Samantha observed as Shining came to the door, demanding attention. She ran her hand along the mare's smooth neck. "I think it's time we started exercising her."

Mandy looked hopefully at Samantha. "I can

help tack her, and groom her after you ride."

"You can help ride her," Samantha told Mandy with a grin. "You're strong enough and a very good rider. I think it would be good for both of you. With your help, we can train her to be a nice saddle horse."

Mandy's jaw dropped slightly, and she turned to Shining. "Did you hear that, girl?" she asked. "I get to help retrain you."

Shining pressed her nose at Mandy and snorted softly.

"I think she likes the idea," Samantha said.

"So do I," Mandy said. "So do I."

The day Tor went to get Miss Battleship, Yvonne and Gregg were at Whisperwood to help with the scheduled Pony Commandos class. It was the first time Samantha had seen them since they had returned from their trip, and Yvonne chattered excitedly about the wonderful time they had had. Mandy, who wanted to be at the farm when Tor brought the new mare home, was saddling Zorro. Samantha smiled to herself as she watched the girl tack the pony.

"Italy was fantastic," Yvonne told Samantha as she saddled Milk Dud. She looked across the arena, where Gregg was talking to Mr. Nelson. "We've already decided we're going back for our anniversary." She checked Milk Dud's girth. "Aren't you looking forward to taking a vacation with Tor?"

Samantha thought of her own canceled honeymoon plans and shook her head. "We're not taking one," she said, then explained about how they had paid for the mare Tor was picking up. "But I'm glad we got her," she said quickly as Yvonne gave her a horrified look.

"Miss Battleship, huh?" Yvonne said, clipping a lead onto Milk Dud's bridle. "Maybe you should rename her Missed the Caribbean."

"Very funny," Samantha said, untying Lollipop as Beth and Janet led the group of students into the arena. "She's a beautiful horse, Yvonne. With her bloodlines, Tor and I will have a good start for our farm."

"Yeah, but you get only one honeymoon," Yvonne said, shaking her head. "I hate to see you miss the trip of a lifetime."

She led Milk Dud to where the eager students were waiting, leaving Samantha to follow with Lollipop, Yvonne's words running through her mind.

The class was over and the horses put away by

the time Tor returned to Whisperwood with his truck and trailer. Mandy was waiting by the barn door, eager to see the new horse. When Tor led her from the trailer, Mandy caught her breath. "She's beautiful," she said as the mare arched her neck and pranced a little, eyeing her new surroundings.

Samantha nodded in agreement as the chestnut mare raised her head and flared her nostrils, taking in the strange smells around her. She whinnied loudly, and when an answering whinny came from one of the turnouts, she snapped her head in that direction.

"She's talking to Top Hat," Samantha said. The big white gelding trotted to the fence, his head high, his ears pricked in their direction, his eyes fixed on the mare. He whinnied again, and Miss Battleship returned the call.

"I wonder how they'd get along," Tor mused, stroking the mare's neck as she looked around Whisperwood.

"We could put her next to him," Samantha suggested. "They might just hit it off."

Tor led the mare to Top Hat's turnout, and the two horses sniffed noses. Miss Battleship released a shrill squeal, and Top Hat took a step back, his eyes wide. Then he took a cautious step closer to the fence.

Samantha held her breath while Miss Battleship took in the gelding's scent, and when the mare lowered her head, relaxing, Samantha sighed.

"I think they'll be fine," Tor said as the two horses stood nose to nose, only the rail fence between them. He let Miss Battleship into the adjoining turnout, and for several minutes they watched as the two Thoroughbreds trotted up and down the fence line side by side. When the mare finally settled down and began sampling the grass underfoot, Tor smiled and nodded.

"We're going to have a good time with her," he predicted.

Samantha rested her forearms on the top rail and gazed at Miss Battleship. "I think so, too," she said, trying to get Yvonne's comment out of her mind. *I'm not sorry we got her,* she told herself. *Even if we can't make a steeplechaser out of her, she's still going to be a top-notch broodmare.*

A few minutes later, Mrs. Jarvis arrived at Whisperwood to pick up Mandy.

"I have so much to tell you," Mandy told her mother as they walked to their car. "I've been doing the most incredible things with Shining. . . ." Her voice faded as she climbed into the sedan, waving good-bye to Samantha and Tor as her mother drove away.

Tor looked at Samantha. "She isn't limping at all anymore," he said.

"I know." Samantha smiled. "And she's doing great things with Shining. They're both making incredible progress." She glanced at her watch. "I need to get back to Whitebrook," Samantha told Tor. "I have chores to do."

"I'll walk you to your car," Tor said. As they crossed the yard he caught Samantha by the arm and stopped her, then looked at her intently. "Are you sure you're okay with using all that money to take a chance on that mare? We can take her back, you know. It isn't too late to change our minds."

Samantha stared up at him for a moment. Was Tor regretting the decision to buy the mare? But as she looked into his eyes, she knew he wanted the horse. "We're not taking her back," she said firmly. "I'm glad we got her. It's going to work out fine. I'm sure of it."

"But I don't want to cheat you out of a honeymoon," Tor said.

"We bought her together," Samantha reminded him. "She's our first investment in our own breeding farm."

"So you don't have any regrets?"

"None," Samantha said. "We're keeping her, and

that's that." She opened her car door. "We can always take a trip later, right?"

"Just not right after the wedding," Tor said.

"I really don't care if we never leave Kentucky," Samantha said, smiling at her fiancé. "As long as I'm with you, life is going to be great."

8

"LOOK AT ALL THESE DRESSES," SAMANTHA SAID, STARING at the rows of wedding gowns that filled the Bridal Shoppe. "I never realized how many different kinds of wedding dresses there were to choose from." Rack after rack of gowns filled the store, in colors ranging from the purest white to the softest yellow. Toward the back of the store were rows of bridesmaid dresses in a rainbow of colors and dozens of styles.

Samantha pressed her hands to her head as she took in the huge display. "I couldn't pick one of these over another!" she exclaimed, fighting the urge to turn and flee the store. "Can't I just get married in jeans?"

"Absolutely not," Beth said firmly. "That's why

I'm here. We're going to make sure you get the right dress."

"Good," Samantha said. "Because I don't have a clue as to what would be right for me."

It seemed to Samantha that she tried on a hundred dresses before Beth and the saleslady gave their nods of approval when she came out of the dressing room in a floor-length dress. Samantha twirled around so they could see the back of the dress she had put on. The full skirt rustled softly, lightly brushing the ground as she crossed the floor to where Beth and the clerk were sitting. Layers of ruffled, lace-trimmed petticoats showed with each step she took. The lace inlays on the fitted bodice matched the petticoats, and the dress reminded Samantha of the women's clothing in movies she had seen about the Old West. "Is it too snug in the top?" she asked, glancing down at herself self-consciously.

"It's perfect," the salesclerk said. "Now to pick a veil to go with it." She brought out several headpieces, and finally Beth and Samantha agreed on a short veil of sheer fabric and lace that matched the dress. "No gloves with this dress," the woman said, looking at Samantha's hands. "But it would be a good idea to get a professional manicure."

Samantha wanted to hide her hands with their

ragged nails behind her back. She didn't think the saleswoman would understand what she put her hands through every day: feeding, grooming, and bathing the horses, cleaning the barns and tack. The whole idea of horse-keeping didn't seem to be part of this world, with the hushed, romantic music playing over the speakers and the store's life-size mannequins dressed in the finest fabrics, vacant looks on their painted faces.

"I think we're done," Samantha said. But when Beth shook her head, she slumped a little. "Not yet?" she asked. "I thought we could go get some lunch, then go home. I'm more worn out from trying on dresses than from a full day of working with the horses."

Beth walked over and lifted a corner of the skirt, pointing at the sneakers Samantha was wearing. "You're not getting married in tennis shoes," she said.

"I have the shoes from Yvonne's wedding," Samantha replied. "They'll work just fine."

"I had something else in mind," Beth replied. "We're going shoe shopping now."

When Beth had the clerk in the shoe department bring out a pair of white lace-up boots, Samantha laughed and nodded. "I couldn't get any closer to paddock boots than that," she said.

"They go well with the dress," the clerk agreed. As soon as Samantha found a pair that fit, the clerk rang them up, and Samantha felt giddy with relief as they left the mall. "I'm glad we found the right dress," she said. "I don't think I could spend another day shopping like that."

"You won't have to," Beth told her, leading the way to the car.

"Thanks for your help, Beth," Samantha said. "I couldn't have picked out the dress and shoes on my own. I would have been lost in there without you."

"Flattering me like that will get me to buy you lunch," Beth said, opening the back door of her car so that Samantha could deposit her packages on the seat.

After a lunch of sweet-and-sour pork, almond chicken, and fried rice at a Chinese restaurant in downtown Lexington, Samantha waited for Beth to read her fortune cookie before she opened hers.

"Mine says 'Happiness will always surround you,'" Beth read. She looked up at Samantha and grinned. "It already does," she said. "I can't imagine being any happier than I am with my family."

Samantha cracked open her cookie and pulled out the slip of paper. "'Don't let the unexpected throw you,'" she read. She wrinkled her nose and looked across the table at Beth. "That doesn't sound too good," she said. "More like a warning than a fortune."

"It's a play fortune," Beth reminded her. "Don't get superstitious about it, okay?"

Samantha nodded, setting the uneaten cookie down as she rose from her side of the table. "I won't," she said. But she would rather have had Beth's cheerful message.

She followed Beth out of the restaurant in silence, and soon they were headed back for Whitebrook. "How is it that a couple of hours in the barn can seem like minutes, but the same amount of time clothes shopping feels like an eternity?" Samantha mused, yawning tiredly as they drove out of Lexington.

Beth laughed. "I think it's part of Einstein's theory of relativity," she said.

"I guess I missed that one in science class," Samantha said, shaking her head. "I didn't realize Einstein ever went dress shopping."

That evening when the family sat down to dinner, Beth had Samantha bring out the dress to show her father, Cindy, and Kevin.

Kevin shrugged when he saw the dress. "I don't like it," he said. "It means I have to dress up, too, and be quiet for a long time while you and Tor stare at each other. Yuck. Can I eat now?" he asked his mother, eyeing the dish of baked potatoes Beth had set on the table.

"But you get to be in the wedding this time," Beth told him, putting a potato on his plate.

"Oh," Kevin said, looking only slightly interested. "Now can I eat?"

"Pretty," Cindy said. "Is my bridesmaid dress going to be the same style? I like the lace and ruffles."

"We'll get together with Yvonne, Mandy, and Ashleigh to pick those out," Samantha told her. "You have to wear the dresses, so you can get what you like."

"Nice dress, honey," Ian said absently, a glum expression on his usually cheerful face.

"Is something wrong?" Beth asked, frowning at her husband.

"I got some bad news today," Ian said as Samantha draped the dress over a side chair and sat down at the table.

She looked at her father expectantly. "What kind of news?" she asked.

"Len has decided to retire," Ian informed them. "His daughter and her husband want him to move to Indiana to be near them."

Samantha felt a cloud settle over her. "When is he going?" she asked.

"He's leaving at the end of February," Ian told her. "He made a point of that, because he doesn't want to miss your wedding."

Samantha poked at the food on her plate. "Whitebrook won't be the same without him," she said. "Who could possibly take his place?"

She thought of Charlie Burke, the old trainer who had helped Ashleigh bring Wonder from a sickly foal to a Derby-winning racehorse, and had helped her so much with Pride. Even though Charlie had passed away nearly five years earlier, Samantha still expected to see him every time she came around the corner of the barn.

Having Len leave would be an awful loss for Whitebrook. She knew that he had worked many years at the farm and had earned his retirement. She was sure he would be happy to be near his daughter and grandchildren, but she was going to miss the kindly old man terribly.

"Mike is advertising for the position," Ian said. "I don't know how long it will take him to find someone as good as Len."

*   *   *

The holidays sped by, with Samantha and Mandy busy training Shining to do more than accept a rider and run. Tor spent his free time working with Miss Battleship, with the hope that he could teach the mare to combine her racing talents with her jumping skills, making a winning steeplechase horse out of her.

One January afternoon when Samantha returned to Whitebrook after a busy day at Whisperwood, she hurried out to the broodmare barn to take care of her chores. Len and Mike were standing in the barn aisle with a man Samantha had never seen before.

"Sammy," Mike said, "I'd like you to meet George Ballard. He's going to be the new manager of the stallion barn."

"Oh." She smiled at Mr. Ballard and extended her hand, then looked at Len. The old man seemed pleased—he gave Samantha a wink, then glanced at George and gave a thumbs-up. Samantha felt better knowing that Len was happy with his replacement, but still, the thought of Len's leaving made her sad.

"Mr. Ballard will move into the cottage behind the barn after Len leaves," Mike said.

"It's a cute little place," George said, nodding. "And Vic seems like he'll be a great roommate. I'm sure I'm going to be happy here."

The week before the wedding, Samantha, Ashleigh, Beth, and Yvonne were sitting in the living room at the McLeans' cottage, wrapping handfuls of birdseed in little satin bags. Christina and Kevin were sitting on the floor, playing with a set of plastic horses.

Christina draped a square of satin over her horse's back, then took one of the filled bags. "Horse feed," she announced, holding the bag up to the horse's nose. "Sky Jumper is hungry."

As she reached for a second bag Ashleigh picked up the pile of filled bags and moved them. "You don't want to overfeed," she told Christina. "Sky Jumper will fly over the moon if you give him too much grain."

"I like the idea of throwing birdseed better than having the guests throw rice," Beth said, taking a handful of ribbons away from Kevin, who was wrapping his plastic horse from head to tail with the white silk. She tied a bag with one of the pieces of ribbon. "All the robins and the sparrows will appreciate your thoughtfulness."

Yvonne tied another little bag shut. "I don't care if you are having a small wedding," she said, setting the bag down on the growing pile of completed favors. "It's still going to be wonderful."

"I love the bridesmaid dresses," Ashleigh said. "It's going to be a wonderful wedding, Sammy."

Samantha nodded, carefully trimming more ribbon to tie the bags. "It's going to be just right for us," she said. But in the back of her mind, she wondered if the small, quiet ceremony was going to be enough. This was Tor's and her special day, and she didn't want to make it less important than what it was.

"If you have some free time tomorrow," Ashleigh said, pouring more seed into a bag, "can you give me a hand with Jazz Dancer? We're thinking of running him when the Keeneland meet opens, and I'd like to do some work with him in the gate before we take him to the track for the stewards to approve him."

"Sure," Samantha said eagerly. She had been so busy with the jumpers at Whisperwood, working with Mandy at retraining Shining, and her regular chores that she hadn't been on a racehorse in months. "But I thought Cindy was helping you with the racehorses."

"She usually does," Ashleigh said. "But she and Max already had plans for tomorrow, and I didn't want to ask her to change them."

By the time Yvonne and Ashleigh left that afternoon, the wedding favors were finished and the table decorations for the reception had been completed.

Tor had invited Samantha to dinner in Lexington, so she left Whitebrook for Whisperwood, looking forward to a quiet evening out.

The next morning, after finishing her chores, Samantha met Ashleigh at the training barn. Ashleigh already had two-year-old Jazz Dancer, a big bay colt by Blues King and out of Precocious, saddled. "Vic has Glory Bee at the track," she said. "Since we're taking Dancer over to Keeneland to run him on the track next week to get his gate approval and get some works recorded, I want to practice with him out of the gate next to another horse."

As part of the rules of Thoroughbred racing, all the horses had to have official times on record as well as their gate approval before they could enter a race. Samantha had helped Ashleigh with gate training several times over the years, and she was glad she was able to spend a little time with her friend working with the young horse, who showed great potential as a distance runner.

Samantha walked with Ashleigh out to the Whitebrook practice track, where Ian had the starting gate set up near the opening in the rail. Vic was standing at the fence holding a lean gray colt. A son of March to Glory and Fleet Goddess, three-year-old Glory Bee swiveled his long neck around so that he could eye Samantha. She held her hand out while the colt sniffed her palm, then she pulled her helmet on and let Vic give her a leg up onto the saddle.

Soon Ashleigh was mounted on Jazz Dancer, and they rode the horses onto the track to warm them up for a few minutes. Since the horses were trained to go from a standstill to a full gallop out of the gate, it was important to let them stretch and loosen up so that they wouldn't strain any muscles when they leaped onto the track. When it came time to load into the practice gate, Glory Bee, who had run in Hialeah during the winter, went into the chute calmly, sniffing the railing while they waited for Ian and Vic to load Jazz Dancer.

But the bay colt balked at the opening. He reared, striking his legs at the gate, fighting to back up instead of going forward into the narrow chute. Samantha watched anxiously as Ashleigh leaned onto his shoulders while Ian held the lead, waiting for Jazz Dancer to bring his weight back down.

"Easy, boy," her father said in a calm voice, stroking the nervous colt's shoulder for a moment. After a couple more failed attempts, Jazz Dancer stood stiff-legged, sniffing cautiously at the tube rails that formed the gate. Ashleigh continued to pet his neck and murmur soothing words to him, and finally Jazz Dancer seemed to tire of fighting. The colt heaved a sigh and marched into the chute without hesitation.

Ashleigh glanced over at Samantha. "Do you think he knows how much easier it would be if he just went in quietly in the first place?" she asked.

Samantha shook her head. "He's pretty rambunctious," she commented, putting her weight forward and tightening her grip on the reins, tangling her fingers in Glory Bee's mane to help her keep her seat when the colt came out of the gate. Beside her, Jazz Dancer began prancing in place, bumping Ashleigh into the side of the gate. He jerked at the reins and pawed the ground nervously, snorting loudly as he danced his hindquarters side to side, trying to turn around in the tight box.

"Let's get going," Ashleigh said to Ian as Jazz Dancer struck out, clanging his shod hoof on the rail. She leaned over Jazz Dancer's shoulders, prepared for the colt to shoot out of the gate when it opened.

Ian gave Vic the signal, and the groom released the gates. Samantha focused forward as Glory Bee surged onto the track. After a couple of strides she started to pull him up, glancing beside her to see how

Ashleigh and Jazz Dancer had done. But she was alone on the track.

She quickly brought Glory Bee around, then looked back to see Vic holding Jazz Dancer's lead and Ashleigh lying on the ground, Ian crouched over her.

9

SAMANTHA JUMPED FROM GLORY BEE'S BACK, TERRIFIED BY the sight of Ashleigh on the ground. But as she hurried back to the gate she could hear Ashleigh talking to Ian, which eased some of her fear.

"Is Jazz Dancer okay?" Ashleigh asked, craning her neck to check on the colt.

"He's fine," Ian said, resting a hand on her shoulder. "What about you?"

"I think I did something to my back when I came off," Ashleigh said weakly. "I felt it pop."

"Then you shouldn't try to move," Ian said. "I'll have Vic call the medics." Ian looked up at the groom, who handed Samantha Jazz Dancer's lead, then took off for the barn at a run.

"I'll tell Mike to get out here," Vic called over his shoulder.

Samantha looked down at Ashleigh's pale face, and her hands started to tremble as she gripped the colts' reins with white-knuckled fists.

Ashleigh offered Samantha a crooked grin. "Don't look so worried," she said. "I'm not paralyzed or anything." She looked up at Jazz Dancer and grimaced. "He went sideways as he came out of the gate," she told Samantha. "He caught his shoulder and went down, and he rolled right over me."

"You go put the horses up," Ian said to Samantha. "I'll stay here with Ashleigh."

Samantha hesitated for a moment, not wanting to leave Ashleigh, but there was nothing she could do to help, so she led the colts back to the barn, trying to convince herself that Ashleigh was fine. But she had a sick feeling that her friend was hurt more than she was letting on.

Len met her at the barn door and took Jazz Dancer's lead. "Vic told me," he said, frowning at the colt. "With the excellent breeding you have, I'd expect better from you," he told the horse, then looked at Samantha. "I'll take care of this rascal while you put Glory Bee up."

By the time Samantha had finished taking care of

the colt and returned to the track, the medics already had Ashleigh in the back of the ambulance. Mike was climbing into the back of the van.

"We'll see you at the hospital," Ian told Mike as the medic shut the rear doors. He turned to Samantha as the ambulance drove away. "Beth has Christina at the house with Kevin," he said. "We can go straight to the hospital."

A couple of hours later Samantha was sitting with Ian in the waiting room at the hospital. The dull green walls and strong smell of antiseptic cleanser filled her senses as she sat on the edge of the vinyl upholstered sofa, watching the clock. Ian patted her knee. "Ashleigh is going to be fine," he reassured her.

She gave her father a thin smile. "I hope so," she said, squeezing her knees against her tightly clenched hands.

Mike had gone into the emergency room with Ashleigh, and time seemed to drag as Samantha waited tensely for the doctor's report. When Mike finally came into the lounge, Samantha jumped to her feet. "Is she going to be all right?" she asked.

Mike nodded, but his expression was serious. "She fractured a vertebra," he told them. "It's going to take a while to heal, but she's going to be okay.

Only," he added, "the doctor strongly advised that she not race anymore. And I agree."

Samantha exhaled a pent-up breath. Ashleigh was going to be all right, and that was all that mattered.

"When can she come home?" Ian asked.

"Tomorrow," Mike said. "But she's not to be up and around for several days." He looked at Samantha. "She asked for you," he said, stepping into the hall so that he could point out the entrance to Ashleigh's room.

Samantha hurried down the aisle, her shoes squeaking loudly on the linoleum floor. She passed the nurses' station and stepped out of the way as an orderly wheeled a gurney toward a bank of elevators. Slipping into Ashleigh's room, she forced a bright smile, trying not to show how much it upset her to see Ashleigh lying in the hospital bed.

"I guess you need a new attendant for the wedding," Ashleigh said, waving her hand at the blue hospital gown she was wearing. "I don't think I'll be doing much for a few weeks."

Samantha immediately shook her head. "We can postpone the wedding," she said. "I don't want to get married until you're able to be in the wedding."

Ashleigh sighed. "You don't have to do that, Sammy," she said. "The Townsends spoiled it for you once. Don't let me ruin your plans a second time."

"You aren't spoiling anything," Samantha said, narrowing her eyes at Ashleigh. "Don't worry about it."

"I'll be upset if you cancel on my account," Ashleigh said. "It isn't fair to you and Tor."

Samantha patted Ashleigh's arm. "You just need to relax and recover. You look pretty beat right now."

Ashleigh nodded. "I am a little tired," she said. "Whatever medication they gave me for the pain is really kicking in." She closed her eyes, then opened them again. "Did Mike tell you?" she asked. "I'm not supposed to race anymore."

"But you can still ride, right?" Samantha asked.

Ashleigh nodded. "Just not on the track," she said, then smiled faintly. "I'm all right with that. I've had lots of great years as a jockey."

She closed her eyes again, and Samantha stood by the bed until Ashleigh's deep, even breathing told her that Ashleigh was asleep. When Samantha left the room, her mind was racing with the things she needed to do to cancel the wedding. She knew Tor would understand, but there was a lot to do to change the plans again.

Mike rode home with Ian and Samantha, all three

of them quiet. Samantha sat in the backseat, lost in thought. No one would be upset that the wedding had to be postponed. That was the least of anyone's worries right now. From where she sat, Samantha could see Mike's profile and the stress lines around his eyes and mouth. She wished there was something she could do to help, but the only thing that Ashleigh needed at the moment was time to heal.

When they reached Whitebrook, Ian put a hand on Mike's arm before he exited the car. "Christina can stay with us, of course," he said. "You take care of Ashleigh."

"I will," Mike replied. "I'm going to call Ashleigh's parents. Derek and Elaine would be upset with me if I didn't let them know what happened. Then I'll head back to the hospital," he said.

"Call if you need anything," Ian said.

Mike nodded. "I will," he said. "You can count on it."

When Samantha got to the cottage, Beth had Kevin and Christina at the kitchen table, coloring pictures. She glanced up when Samantha walked into the kitchen, a worried look on her face.

"I need to call Tor," Samantha informed her. "I'm not getting married until Ashleigh can be by my side at the altar."

"I expected you would say that," Beth said, picking a folder up from the counter. She held it out to Samantha. "Here's the guest list and the numbers for the florist, the caterer, and the minister," she said. "You'll need to let them know, too."

After talking with Tor, Samantha made the rest of the calls, canceling all the wedding arrangements. Then she wandered out to the barn, where Len was finishing the evening chores.

"Ashleigh will be fine," the old stable hand assured her.

Samantha tried to smile at him. "I know," she said. "But it seems like every time we make wedding plans, something goes wrong." She felt a cloud of gloom settle over her. "Maybe I'm just not supposed to get married," she said glumly.

Len raised his eyebrows. "Things happen," he said calmly, covering her hand with his large one. "It has nothing to do with you and Tor getting married."

"It sure feels that way," Samantha replied. "Maybe I was just meant to stay single and spend all my time working with the horses."

Len propped his fists on his hips and scowled at her, shaking his head firmly. "Quit feeling sorry for yourself and give me a hand here," he said. "Everything is going to work out just fine. You're not going to let a few little setbacks keep you from being happy with Tor for the rest of your life, are you?"

Samantha gave him a startled look. "I'm not—" Then she caught herself, remembering her fortune cookie: *Don't let the unexpected throw you.* She thought about all the things that had happened since Gregg and Yvonne's wedding, and nodded slowly. She was letting things throw her, thinking that everything that went wrong was because of the wedding. "You're right," she said, picking up a pan of feed. "I am going to be happy with Tor, no matter what happens." She grinned at Len. "Now let's get these horses fed."

Helping Len with the chores lifted her spirits, and by the time she went back to the cottage for dinner, Samantha was feeling upbeat and hopeful. Tor's truck was parked in front of the cottage, and when she went inside, the delicious smell of lasagna wafted from the kitchen. Tor was in the living room, Kevin and Christina snuggled up on either side of him on the sofa. Samantha stood in the doorway, watching him read out loud from one of Kevin's storybooks, and she felt a rush of warmth and fondness for Tor.

When he looked up and caught her eye, he smiled and winked at her. "We're right in the middle of *The*

Misadventures of Perky Pony," he said. "Would you like to join us?"

All the worries Samantha had about everything going wrong if she and Tor set another wedding date faded completely, and she smiled back. "I'll go wash up and see if I can help Beth with dinner," she told him. "It looks like you have things under control here."

The second wedding date passed, and Samantha tried not to think about it. Len left the farm, promising that when a new wedding date was set, he would come back to visit. As the trees began to bud and the weather grew warmer, Samantha couldn't help but wonder what she and Tor would be doing right now if they were already married. Would they have found a home of their own, or would they have stayed with Mr. Nelson at Whisperwood, training the jumpers and teaching lessons together?

Ashleigh was doing better daily. She made a point of visiting the barn, but no one would let her lift so much as a bridle or do anything more with the horses than pet them.

"I'm going to go crazy being treated like an

invalid," she told Samantha one day. She rubbed her back and sighed. "I'm starting to feel like an old woman," she said with a wry chuckle. "I can get around, but it sure takes a lot out of me."

"You're far from old, and you'll be back in the saddle before you know it," Samantha reassured her. "Just not on the racetrack."

Ashleigh nodded. "I know, and I'd be really upset if that was all I had to look forward to, but with my family, and working with all the horses in training, I have a wonderful life without being a jockey."

For the next couple of days Samantha was busy working with Shining, and she watched with satisfaction as Mandy rode the mare around the outdoor arena. Shining responded willingly to Mandy's cues, moving smoothly from a walk to a trot and into a collected canter. Mandy looked very comfortable on the mare, sitting tall in the saddle, her back straight and her chin up.

Tor came to the fence and watched for a few minutes. "I'm impressed," he told Samantha. "Both of them are doing so well."

Samantha nodded. "When Shining was racing and Mandy was crippled, I never imagined anything like this. But they look great together, don't they?"

Mandy brought Shining out of the arena, her face beaming. "Isn't she the most perfect horse in the world?" she asked Tor, patting the mare's neck. "I'm so lucky to be able to ride her."

Tor nodded. "The two of you are pretty awesome," he told Mandy.

She turned to Samantha. "Thanks so much for letting me work with her," she said. "I'm starting to feel like a real rider now." She gave Shining's lead a gentle pull. "Come on, girl," she said. "Let's get you untacked. You've earned a really good grooming today."

She walked away, and Samantha watched her lead Shining to the barn.

"I thought I'd saddle Miss Battleship, and you can take Sierra out for a ride with us," Tor said. "With all this wonderful spring sunshine, the weather is perfect for an afternoon on horseback."

Soon Samantha and Tor had their horses ready. Tor had been riding Miss Battleship regularly, conditioning her muscles and trying to develop her racing technique to the point where she could succeed in a steeplechase. So far her progress was slow, and Tor was getting discouraged. But in spite of her limits as a steeplechaser, the mare still had an impressive build, and her disposition made her a pleasure to work with.

They warmed the horses up in the outdoor arena, and Samantha watched Tor take the mare over a few fences. Miss Battleship cleared the four- and five-foot rails easily, arching her neck and cantering gracefully around the course between jumps.

"She makes a wonderful show jumper," Samantha commented. "But then when she's on the flat track and focused on running, she's a rocket. I wish she could put the two together. We'd have an awesome mare to race."

"I know," Tor said. "But nothing I do seems to help her. I'm afraid we spent our honeymoon money on a dud as far as getting her to win a steeplechase."

Samantha whipped her head to the side and stared at Tor. "No, we didn't," she said firmly, looking from Tor to the mare. "Even if she isn't going to be a winner on the track, she'll make a good broodmare. Her bloodlines and her talent, combined with the right sire, could produce a steeplechaser that would make the world sit up and take notice."

"Okay, okay," Tor said. "You've convinced me."

They rode in silence for several minutes, the tense moment passing. Then Tor twisted in his saddle and looked straight at Samantha. "It'll be nice when we have our own place," he said. "I know about training, but we've never run a breeding program. That's going to have to be your area of expertise."

Samantha nodded. "With what I've learned living at Whitebrook, and with Ashleigh and Mike's help, we'll do great," she agreed. "We have Lucky Chance and Miss Battleship, and in time we'll build up more of our own breeding stock." She paused. "But we need to get settled on a place and starting working at it."

Tor nodded. "I guess we'll just have to wait," he said. "But if we put off the wedding every time something comes up, we may never get around to it."

Samantha looked at him. "Maybe we should just have a quiet civil ceremony," she said. "I don't care if we go to a justice of the peace. We only need two witnesses, and then we can start shopping for a farm of our own."

Tor stared at her. "I thought you wanted a nice wedding," he said. "I don't want to take that away from you."

Samantha shrugged, patting Sierra's neck absently. "We don't need anything fancy," she said. "We need to get started with our own lives."

"Then that's what we'll do," Tor replied. "We

already have the license, so we can get married whenever you say so."

"The sooner the better," Samantha said. Tor was right. If they kept waiting for things to be just right, they might never get married.

10

"WHAT DO YOU MEAN, WE CAN'T GO ON WEDNESDAY?" Samantha asked Yvonne. She pressed the phone receiver to her ear and sighed. "We have it all set up. You and Gregg are going to meet Tor and me at the courthouse so you can be our witnesses. You can't back out now."

"I just can't make it," Yvonne said, sounding a little abrupt. "Next week will work better. After putting things off this long, a few more days won't hurt you."

Samantha was surprised by Yvonne's attitude. She had thought her friend would be more understanding, but Yvonne didn't seem concerned in the least about making Samantha change her plans again.

Samantha exhaled heavily. "Okay," she said. There was no use arguing with Yvonne. "I'll call Tor and let him know. But next week you won't have any excuses, right?"

"I promise," Yvonne said. "Right now I have to go. I'll talk to you later."

Samantha hung up the phone and called Whisperwood to tell Tor the news that Yvonne and Gregg couldn't be their witnesses if they got married this week.

Mr. Nelson answered the phone in the barn office. "Tor's got a class going right now," he informed Samantha. "Can I give him a message?"

Samantha shared the news with Tor's father, then waited for his reaction.

"That's a shame" was all Mr. Nelson said, not sounding at all concerned about the postponed plans.

Samantha frowned as she hung up the phone. The cottage was quiet, and the silence pressed around her. Beth was at work, Cindy had taken Kevin and Christina to the park for the afternoon, and her father was at the barn. Samantha left the house and wandered down to the broodmare barn, where Vic was talking to George Ballard, the new employee. As Samantha drew near, the two men looked up at her and fell silent.

Samantha eyed them warily, wondering what they were talking about that they didn't want her to hear.

"You look a little unhappy," Vic observed.

Samantha forced a smile. "I'm fine," she replied, nodding at Mr. Ballard. She hadn't had much of a chance to get to know the stallion manager, but he seemed nice enough. Maybe when her life was more settled she would spend some time visiting with him, but at the moment she had too much on her mind.

She hurried past the two men and went out to the paddocks, where Lucky Chance was dozing in the warm summer sun. Samantha climbed into the turn-out and crossed the pasture to pet the filly's shiny black neck.

"I'm going to be an old maid," she told Lucky, who sniffed at her hands and pockets, looking for treats. "Maybe Maureen and I will be silly old single ladies together, wearing purple and drinking tea together on the porch. And it makes no difference to you, does it?"

The filly rubbed her cheek against Samantha's shoulder, nearly knocking her off her feet. "I need to spend more time working with you," Samantha said, pushing Lucky's head away. "Your manners are horrible." Lucky Chance tried once again to scratch herself on Samantha, but when Samantha shoved her away a second time, the filly gave up and instead dropped her nose to the ground to nibble at the grass.

Samantha left the turnout and shoved her hands into her pockets as she walked back to the barn, debating whether she should drive over to Whisperwood to talk to Tor. As she started to walk past the office, she heard Mike on the phone.

"That's right," he said. "We'll need at least three farm wagons, and matched draft horses for each wagon. Can you manage that?"

Samantha stood outside the door, frowning. *Horse-drawn wagons? For what?* She started to head inside to ask Mike what he was planning, but as she took a step, Cindy came down the aisle at a jog.

"Sammy," she said breathlessly, "can you give me a hand?"

"Where are Kevin and Christina?" Samantha asked. "I thought you had them out for the afternoon."

"I did," Cindy said. "But when we went by Mona Gardener's, they wanted to stop and see her jumpers. They ended up staying for a special riding lesson. Mona's bringing them home later."

Ashleigh's old school friend Mona taught show jumping at her nearby farm, and Christina took regular lessons with the experienced trainer.

"Now I need a hand." Cindy waved urgently, drawing Samantha away from Mike's office.

"Sure," Samantha said, forgetting about Mike and the horse-drawn wagons as she followed Cindy. Her sister turned and strode back up the aisle. Samantha hurried to catch up as Cindy left the broodmare barn, slowing as they got away from the door. "What's up?" Samantha asked.

"I . . . uh . . . I need . . . um . . . " Cindy stammered, pausing for a moment as she looked around. Then suddenly she started in the direction of the stallion barn. "It's Champion," she said quickly, glancing over her shoulder. "I think there's something wrong with his leg, and I can't find Mr. Ballard to check him out for me."

"I saw him with Vic in the broodmare barn," Samantha said, frowning at Cindy's back.

"But you're here now, so you can help me," Cindy said. "Come on."

Perplexed by Cindy's odd behavior, Samantha followed her into the stallion barn. Champion was in his stall, and Cindy picked up his halter and a stud chain to bring him into the aisle.

"I think he's off on his left hind leg," she said. "Watch him walk, will you?"

Samantha stood in the middle of the aisle and watched closely as Cindy led the stallion up and down the barn.

"He looks fine," Samantha said. "What made you think he was limping?"

"Look again," Cindy urged, leading the horse away one more time.

"He's fine," Samantha said, feeling a little impatient. The big stallion didn't show the slightest indication of lameness. Samantha walked over to him and ran her hands down each of his legs, then gave Cindy a quizzical look. "He's sound as can be," she said, shaking her head.

"He just didn't look right," Cindy said, turning her attention to the big chestnut horse. Champion nuzzled her, and Cindy stroked his neck. "I worry about him, you know."

"I realize that," Samantha said, not sure if she should be amused or irritated by Cindy's behavior. "But I still don't understand what made you think he had a problem. I'm going up to the house to see Ashleigh. I haven't talked to her since yesterday, and I want to see how she's doing."

"Oh, no," Cindy said, putting Champion back

into his stall. "I need a ride into town, and there's no one around but you."

"What's wrong with your car?" Samantha asked, folding her arms in front of her. "You just came back from driving the kids around."

"I think . . . well, it sort of . . ." Cindy's voice trailed off. "I mean, it needs oil," she said. "I need you to take me to the auto parts store so I can pick up a couple of quarts. Dad would strangle me if I let it run out."

Samantha exhaled, confused by Cindy's strange antics, but she didn't have anything better to do this afternoon, and she didn't have the mental energy to try to figure Cindy out. "Fine," she said. "Let's go."

After they had purchased the oil for Cindy's car, Cindy asked Samantha to take her to the tack store. "I want to look at the new racing saddles," she said. "And I need a new girth. The old one is getting a little worn."

"Why do I get the impression you're up to something?" Samantha asked, eyeing her younger sister suspiciously.

"Who, me?" Cindy widened her eyes, giving Samantha a look of pure innocence. "I just wanted to spend some time with my big sister, that's all. With everything you've been doing, and all the time I've been putting into racing and getting ready to gradu-ate, we don't get to do much together."

Samantha frowned thoughtfully. "Okay," she said. "I'll buy that." But things still didn't quite add up.

Cindy took a frustratingly long time in the tack shop, and finally Samantha hustled her to the check-out. "It shouldn't take an hour to pick out a girth," she said, feeling a little irritated.

Cindy glanced at her watch and nodded. "You're right," she said. "Let's get going." She walked quickly out to the car, leaving Samantha to once again shake her head over Cindy's bizarre actions.

When they returned to Whitebrook, Samantha headed for the cottage. "Can we stop by the main house first?" Cindy asked. "You said you haven't seen Ashleigh in a long time. I'd like to visit her, too."

Samantha started to ask why, then clamped her mouth shut. She didn't want to hear whatever off-the-wall reason Cindy had for going up to the Reeses' house, and she had a hunch it wouldn't make any sense. She parked near the front door, climbed from the car, and walked up the porch. Before she could knock on the door, Cindy darted around her and swung it open, then stepped back with a flourish.

"Surprise!" The chorus of voices from inside

startled Samantha, and she gaped at the roomful of people.

"What in the world is going on here?" she asked, slowly walking into the room. Yvonne, Maureen, Ashleigh's friend Linda March, Mona, Mandy and her mother, Beth, and Ashleigh's mother were sitting in the living room, smiling at her.

"A wedding shower," Yvonne said, crossing the room to grab Samantha by the arm. "You are the hardest person to get out of the way for a few hours so we could get this set up." She tugged Samantha's arm, leading her across the room, then gave her a gentle push into an empty chair.

Samantha gazed around at all the people gathered in the Reeses' living room and shook her head. "You shouldn't have done this," she said. "We're not even going to have a real wedding now. We're just going to have a civil ceremony. I don't need a shower."

"Oh, yes, you do," Ashleigh said from where she was sitting next to her mother.

Elaine Griffin smiled at Samantha. "It's all arranged," she said. "We're not going to let you get married in a cold courtroom without your friends and family there."

"Who needs a wedding planner when you have

all these friends to take care of it for you?" Beth asked. "We've got everything taken care of, Sammy."

"We're having the wedding here, next week," Cindy announced, grinning broadly. "And we're going to have it on horseback."

11

"There," Yvonne said, stepping back to examine the veil she had fastened on top of Samantha's hair. "I think you're ready to go." She picked up a hand mirror and held it up so that Samantha could see herself. "You look absolutely beautiful, Sammy."

Samantha stared at the woman in the mirror, hardly able to believe it was herself she was looking at. The subtle makeup Yvonne had applied made her green eyes appear larger and wider than normal, and delicate touches of color on her cheeks and lips enhanced the angles of her face. "Wow," she said. "I feel like a princess in a fairy tale." She ran her hands down the full skirt of her wedding gown, then looked at Ashleigh, who was standing near the bedroom door. The pale, rose-colored dress Ashleigh wore was much plainer than Samantha's ruffle and lace-decorated gown, but the matron of honor still looked fabulous. "Thank you for making all this happen," Samantha said, smiling at her friend.

"I'm just happy I was able to do a few things to help you and Tor along," Ashleigh said. "And I definitely didn't do it alone. You have lots of friends, Sammy."

There was a knock on the door, but as Samantha started to rise, Ashleigh held her hand up. "It might be Tor," she said. "And we know it's bad luck for the groom to see the bride before the wedding. I'll get it." Ashleigh opened the door a crack and peeked around the corner, then stepped back to swing it open wide. Ian came into the room, looking dignified and handsome in his dark suit.

When he saw Samantha, he stopped, his eyes wide. "You are breathtaking, sweetheart," he said. "Tor is the luckiest man on the planet."

"Thanks, Dad," Samantha said, feeling her cheeks go warm as her father gazed at her.

"You remind me so much of your mother," he said with a sigh. "I only wish she could have been here to see this day."

"Me too," Samantha said.

Ian dug into his pocket and held out a small package. "I'd like you to wear this," he said, pressing the box into Samantha's hand.

When she opened it, she gasped, lifting a delicate gold bracelet studded with emeralds and sapphires from the box. "This was Mom's," she said, showing it to Ashleigh.

"I bought it for your mother as a wedding present," Ian said. "Now it's yours."

"Will you put it on me?" Samantha asked her father.

Samantha could feel his hands trembling slightly as he fastened the clasp, and she saw him blinking rapidly.

"Thank you, Dad," she said softly, then wrapped her arms around his neck.

Ian gave her a light hug, then held her at arm's length. "We don't want to rumple your dress," he said, visibly struggling to hold back the tears that welled at the corners of his eyes. "I'll see you at the altar," he told her, digging a tissue from his pocket as he hurried from the room.

"Something old and something blue," Samantha said, gazing at the bracelet.

"I have something for you to borrow, but it's waiting outside," Ashleigh said with a mysterious smile.

Cindy, Maureen, and Mandy met them in the living room, and Samantha took a moment to admire her bridesmaids, all wearing dresses of the same light rose color as Ashleigh's matron of honor dress. Samantha followed the five attendants out of the house, stopping short when she reached the edge of the porch. She stared in amazement at the incredible scene in front of her.

Close to the barn, rows of horse trailers were parked, and she swept her eyes across the lawn, taking in dozens of guests on horseback. Families with small children, and the older visitors, were settling into wagons pulled by massive bay Clydesdales. Stunned by the activity in front of her, Samantha snapped her head around to stare at Ashleigh.

"When Cindy said we were having the wedding on horseback, I didn't realize you meant the guests, too," she said. "How did you pull this off? It's incredible."

Ashleigh smiled and shrugged. "Everyone we know is so passionate about their horses, it seemed like the right way for you and Tor to get married," she said. "I made a few phone calls, and the word spread like wildfire."

A large trellis covered with white roses stood at one end of the lawn, and Samantha could see the minister, seated on a tall bay, waiting for the procession. She heard the faint, delicate sound of harp music, and looked around to see the harpist sitting near the wagons full of guests.

Samantha gazed at the breathtaking scene, imprinting it on her mind. "I will remember this forever," she told her friends.

"Here's your ride now," Mandy said excitedly as Ian came around the corner astride one of the pony horses, leading Ashleigh's Wonder and Wonder's Pride, their copper coats gleaming like a new penny. Both horses wore sidesaddles, but a garland of white roses was draped over Pride's glossy neck, and white satin ribbons covered his bridle and reins. Ashleigh looked at Samantha. "Would you like to borrow a horse?" she asked.

"Oh, my gosh," Samantha said, pressing her hand to her mouth. "I can't believe you did all this."

"I'd do it again in a second," Ashleigh said sincerely. "I'm so happy for you, Sammy."

Cindy stepped off the porch as Vic strode up to the house with Yvonne's jumper, Cisco, Shining, and Honor Bright, one of Cindy's favorite racehorses.

Samantha walked down the steps and raised her hand to touch Pride's silky nose. "You're going to be in my wedding," she said.

As Samantha and her entourage started down the hill on their horses, the crowd fell silent. The only sounds Samantha could hear were the stomping of horses' hooves and the strings of the harp. They rode up the wide swath of grass the guests had left open, and ahead of them, Samantha could see Tor on Miss Battleship, and beside him, Mike on Jazzman.

The ride seemed almost dreamlike, sitting on the sidesaddle and moving to Pride's prancing steps. When they reached the arch of flowers, Samantha stopped her horse, positioning him so that she and Tor were side by side.

She smiled broadly when she saw Len sitting in one of the wagons, with George Ballard beside him. She swept her eyes over the crowd, seeing so many people who were dear to her and who cared enough to help Ashleigh create the most unforgettable wedding possible. Ashleigh was right. She did have a lot of friends.

She turned to glance at Tor, who reached out and caught her hand in his, and the minister began to speak.

The ceremony went quickly, and soon the guests who had brought their horses were taking the animals back to the trailers so that they could visit and eat.

"It's time for our dance," Tor told her as Vic led their horses away. To Samantha's surprise, Len walked over to the musician, then smiled at Samantha. "I have something to give you," he said. "I usually sing only in church, but today this is for you."

The harpist strummed the strings, and Len started to sing an old jazz tune. As Tor waltzed Samantha around the lawn to Len singing "What a Wonderful World," she sighed happily. "I don't care about not having a honeymoon," she told Tor. "I've been given the most unbelievable day of my life, and it's more than enough." She hummed along with the song for a moment, then tilted her head back to smile up at her husband. "He's right," she said. "It is a wonderful world."

Tor smiled down at her and nodded. "Yes, Mrs. Nelson," he said. "It is most definitely a wonderful world."

After several more dances, Samantha cut the wedding cake, and people gathered close to offer toasts to the bride and groom.

"Now it's time to open your gifts," Beth informed Samantha and Tor, indicating a table piled with packages wrapped in silver, pink, and white papers. Mandy sat down with a pad of paper to write down who had given what gift, so that Samantha could properly thank people.

The first large package Samantha unwrapped was a suitcase, and she frowned at it, perplexed. "This is from your parents," she told Mandy, who nodded, scribbling a note on her paper.

"Matching travel kits," Tor said, giving Samantha a puzzled look. He leaned close to her. "Maybe not everyone knew that we canceled our trip," he murmured.

But as they opened present after present, each one had something to do with traveling, and Samantha didn't know whether to laugh or cry.

"There's one more," Mandy said, pointing at an envelope sitting on the table.

Samantha picked it up and handed it to Tor. His eyes widened when he unfolded the sheet of paper inside, and he turned to Samantha, his jaw slack.

"We may not be taking that trip to the Caribbean," he said, holding out the note. "But we are going to spend a month in Ireland, on an equestrian holiday!"

12

"THAT'S THE LAST OF THE BOXES," CINDY ANNOUNCED, dusting her hands on her jeans.

Samantha jumped a bit, startled back to the present from her reverie of years long past. She looked around the room, amazed to see how much her friends had accomplished while she was talking.

"Wow," she said, eyeing the few boxes that were left. "I feel bad now. I was sitting here blabbing while you all kept working away."

"I didn't mind a bit," Christina said, grinning at Samantha. "I'm so glad I got to hear those stories."

Samantha pointed at the remaining boxes. "Those are all photos and bits of memorabilia we want to keep, right?" she asked Tor. When he nodded, she smiled. "We can spend a few quiet evenings sorting through them and making up some albums. That way we can go through them with the baby when she's old enough and tell her all these stories."

"You mean he," Tor corrected her, his eyes twinkling.

"Maybe them," Ashleigh said, looking at Samantha's stomach. "I don't mean to sound rude, Sammy, but you are awfully big around the middle."

Samantha pressed her hands to her stomach and laughed. "I have to go in for a checkup next week," she said. "If the doctor hears two different heartbeats, you'll be the first to know."

"Could it really be twins?" Christina asked, wide-eyed.

Tor shrugged. "You never know," he said.

"That would be so cool," Christina said, clapping her hands together. "Two Whisperwood kids."

Samantha looked around the room again and nodded. "At least we have a room for them," she said. "Now all I need to do is paint and decorate."

"Oh, no, you don't," Ashleigh and Cindy said in unison.

"We're coming back to finish the room this weekend," Christina said. "Now that we can get to the walls, we're going to turn this into an official nursery."

"Thank you," Samantha said gratefully. "You guys are the best friends I could ever wish for."

Ashleigh glanced at her watch. "Right now it's time for the three fairy godmothers to head for home," she said. "It's my turn to cook dinner."

"And I want to call Parker before it gets too late," Christina said. "The time difference between here and England completely throws me."

Cindy nodded. "I need to swing by the clothing bank, and then I'm going to meet Ben in Lexington for dinner," she announced.

After the three visitors had left, Samantha and Tor returned to the almost empty nursery. Samantha listened to the call of a bird in a tree outside the window, and in the distance a horse whinnied. "It's so peaceful here," she said. "I can't imagine living anywhere else."

"There was a time you didn't want to leave Ireland," Tor reminded her.

"I know," she said. "But things have a way of working out the way they're supposed to."

"Everything has worked out just right," Tor agreed.

"I am the luckiest person in the world," Samantha said with a happy sigh. "Look at all the work those three did. We have such great friends and family."

Tor stood behind Samantha, resting his chin on her head as they gazed through the doorway. "We are very lucky," he said. "We have good friends, we've made a wonderful home for a child, and we're doing what we love. And," he added, "I have you, and that makes me the luckiest man on earth."

Man o' War during his retirement in Lexington, Kentucky.

Man o' War

1917-1947

Man o' War was purchased for $5,000 at the 1918 Saratoga yearling sale. His new owner, Samuel Riddle, knew that if the big chestnut colt didn't pan out as a racehorse, he had the size to be a jumper. Nonetheless, during his two-year racing career on the flat track, Big Red won twenty of his twenty-one races and placed second in one.

In spite of racing with weights of up to 138 pounds, more than any other Thoroughbred his age had ever carried, Man o' War still won his races easily, setting track records that remained unbeaten until the 1970s.

Man o' War was retired as a three-year-old because Sam Riddle was concerned that the handicappers would continue to increase the weights the colt carried until they broke him.

At stud, Man o' War sired sixty-four stakes winners, as well as several renowned jumpers, including champion show jumper Holystone, Maryland Hunt Cup winner Blockade, and Grand National steeplechase winner Battleship. When Man o' War passed away in 1947, he was buried in a special grave at the Kentucky Horse Park; the memorial still attracts thousands of visitors every year. As his longtime groom, Will Harbut, was frequently quoted as saying about this incomparable Thoroughbred, "He was the mostest horse."

Mary Newhall spent her childhood exploring back roads and trails on horseback with her best friend. She now lives with her family and horses on Washington State's Olympic Peninsula. Mary has written novels and short stories for both adults and young adults.